ROCKY POINT LEGACY
Rocky Point Series, Book One

BARBARA MCMAHON

Chapter One

Gillian Parker parked her rental car at the curb. Glancing around, she tried to absorb every sight immediately—the clapboard homes on the side street; the weathered fronts on the buildings closer to the ocean. The spaciousness of the main street and the delightful flower designs painted on the old iron street lights.

She was utterly charmed.

Rocky Point, Maine, had only been a dot on the map before today. Now she sat in her car in the heart of the small New England town.

She stepped from the car and locked the door. Not that there was anything in the car itself. Her suitcase was in the trunk. But habits were habits.

Walking to the front of the café, she involuntarily smiled again noticing the quaint decor. Flower boxes lined the bottom of the large windows, with colorful blooms already spilling over the edge. The outside had been painted recently and gave a friendly feel of welcome to the establishment.

She opened the door and walked in, her high heels rapping on the hardwood floors. The waitresses carried trays of food, weaving through the throng, their pinafore period costumes adding to the charm of the old-time decor, which seemed to make the café a top destination for lunch judging by the crowd.

"Table for one?" a waitress asked, pausing for a moment.

"Yes."

"Follow me, there's a table in the back."

As she followed the waitress Gillian felt the center of all eyes. Conversation seemed to diminish a bit, as she passed, then regained the previous volume.

She'd heard stories about small towns recognizing strangers when they arrived. Judging from the weekday work attire of the folks at the tables, her clothing would also signal something out of the ordinary.

She'd just come from the funeral where she had worn her only black suit. It was a bit dressy for a midweek afternoon.

The waitress waited until she was seated at the small table then handed her the menu. "Our special today is crab cakes. The sisters make the best in town."

Gillian smiled and began to study the menu, wondering who the sisters were. Everything looked delicious. How to decide. Maybe she'd take the waitress's suggestion. The crab was undoubtedly fresh.

Glancing around after she ordered, Gillian smiled at a couple of people when they met her eye. They smiled in return.

She felt almost giddy with excitement. This was her first day in town, and if the Lord willed it, she'd be here until the day she died. Gillian prayed this would become her home.

All things pointed to it.

The crab cakes were fabulous. The fresh fruit compote that accompanied it was a delicious balance. She sipped the tea she'd ordered and wondered if she'd have difficulty finding the house she'd come to claim. From what she'd seen of the town so far, it was laid out in squares, neat and compact and easily navigated.

"How's the lunch?" A woman dressed in a costume similar to Gillian's waitress stopped by the table with a smile.

"Delicious, thanks."

"Glad to hear it. I'm Marcie Evans. I own this place."

"The food is wonderful, and I really like the decor and uniforms."

Marcie smile broadened. "So glad to hear that, too. You're not from around here."

"That obvious, huh?" Gillian asked, almost laughing.

She felt as out of place here as she would in a chorus line at a Vegas show.

"I was born and raised here, so I know everyone," Marcie said.

"I'm Gillian Parker, and no, I'm not from around here. I'm from Nevada."

"Related to Sophie?"

Gillian nodded.

"I'm so sorry about her death. I missed the funeral because of work. One of my waitresses is out sick today, so I have to fill in. Sophie was wonderful. She will be missed."

Gillian smiled, trying to hide the pang that this young woman had known her great-grandmother when she herself had only learned of her existence after her death—when the lawyer's call had told her she was the beneficiary of Sophie's estate.

"Do you know how to get to Sophie's house? I inherited it."

There, she'd said it aloud.

She had stopped by the lawyer's office briefly after she'd arrived in town. Not wanting to be late to the funeral, the visit had been short. Julian Greene had given her the gist of the legacy and promised to meet with her another day to review things in more detail.

Now that lunch was almost over, Gillian was anxious to see the place she'd inherited. And to begin making plans to move to Maine.

"Better than that," Marcie said with a twinkle in her eye. "Your next-door neighbor is eating lunch here as well. He came here straight from the funeral, too. You can follow him out to the house. It's on a bluff halfway around the cove. Once you know which road to take from town, you'll have no problem finding it. Let me bring Joe over and introduce the two of you."

Marcie wove her way through the tables and went to a booth on the side.

Gillian recognized the man Marcie spoke to as one of the pallbearers at the funeral. He had stood a head above the other men and was much younger.

He glanced over at Gillian and she smiled politely.

He frowned and looked back at Marcie.

So much for neighborliness, she thought. Maybe Marcie had underestimated a neighbor's willingness to help.

"Come on, Joe. It won't hurt a bit. Just have her follow you out of town and point out Sophie's place as you pass. You don't have to do more than meet her and say 'follow me,'" Marcie said to the stubborn man in front of her.

"I'm not interested in getting to know some come-and-go woman who probably plans to sell before Sophie's in the ground good."

Joe frowned at Marcie. It was a good thing no one could read minds. He knew better, but that didn't stop his interest in the stranger. He'd seen her at the church and then wobbling across the lawn in those high heels at the cemetery. He might have thought staying single was the way to go these days, but it didn't make him immune to the attractions of a beautiful woman.

He just hoped he had better sense than to act on that attraction.

"She seems nice," Marcie said.

Joe peered around her and met the gaze of the woman he'd noticed at the funeral and again after she'd walked into the café.

She was stunning. If this weren't Rocky Point, and if he didn't have a daughter to worry about, he might go over and find out if she were as nice as Marcie suggested.

"If she's Sophie's great-granddaughter, why didn't anyone know about her?" he asked.

"I doubt Julian Greene would hand the keys to the house to someone he wasn't convinced was a relative. Better have her there than the house stand empty. Though her arrival is a surprise," Marcie acknowledged.

"We're going to miss Sophie. Her death hit Jenny especially hard."

"I'm sure. She was a good neighbor, and Jenny had the run of her house. Hard as it is to face, we all need to know life on earth is temporary. It's eternal life to look forward to," Marcie said gently.

"I knew Sophie all my life. My folks moved into the house next to hers before I was even born. It won't ever be the same."

Marcie nodded. "Still, she had a nice long life."

"Yes, she had a long life, but how nice it was is anyone's guess. Her husband died during the Depression, her only son died in the Korean War, her grandson disappeared one day after trying to gyp her out of all her money. And she had to work hard to keep going and keep up that house—especially after she retired."

"She had lots of friends, her church work, and I know she thought of you and Jenny as family," Marcie said gently. "You always treated her that way. And she had money enough to hire help when she really needed it."

"I'm going to miss her. It's difficult to imagine what it's going to be like without her next door," Joe said, glancing again at the stranger sitting alone at her table.

His daughter, Jenny, had been devastated when she learned Sophie had died from a fall down her stairs likely caused by a stroke. With both Joe's parents dead, his wife long gone, Sophie had completed their small family.

He studied the stranger for a moment, feeling that kick of interest ramp up a notch. It had been so long since he'd been this interested in someone–he didn't like it. For a moment he felt like he had when he'd been younger—carefree, daring, a bit wild. Her red-gold hair was a riotous, flaming swirl around her head and shoulders. She was tall and slender with legs that seemed to go on forever. The sophisticated black suit was as out of place in Rocky Point as she was.

And he wanted to get to know her. Find out what made her come out of the blue to Rocky Point. Was she planning to stay?

She arrived just as the service in the old church began. Sitting alone, she hadn't shed a tear, nor talked to anyone. She claimed to be Sophie's great-granddaughter. In all the years he'd known Sophie, she'd never said a word about having a great-granddaughter.

The black suit and black shoes should have had her looking like a glorious crow. Black was not her color. Still—it highlighted her creamy complexion, made her blue eyes seem brighter than anyone's and provided a dramatic backdrop for that vibrant hair, which seemed to be a beacon of light capturing pure sunshine.

Would it be flame hot or silky cool to the touch?

Her blue eyes sparkled even at this distance.

Joe was older and wiser now than he'd been when he married Pamela. Now his life was firmly centered in the Lord. He knew that stepping outside of the Lord's will would result in havoc. The years of his tumultuous marriage had proved that. He was content with his life, his work and his small family. But it didn't hurt to look at beauty–and even yearn just a little bit.

"Okay, she can follow me home," he said, turning back to the last of his lunch.

"Gee, be happy, why don't you? It's not as if you have to introduce her around or anything, just show her the house."

"I said all right."

"Then come and meet her. I have other things to do and don't want you taking off before you meet. She might actually be nice."

"Ha."

"Time you moved on, Joe. Get married again, have some more babies. Not every woman's like Pamela," Marcie said with the bluntness of a long-time friend.

"I haven't even met the woman and you're matchmaking?" he asked in astonishment.

Had he given himself away? Not that he was interested in marriage—or even a long-term relationship.

He would settle for admitting to being *curious* about Gillian Parker. That was it.

"No. I just want you to open yourself up to the possibility. You need to find someone to fall in love with, someone who will bring you sunshine and joy. The Lord has the right person in mind, but you need to do your part, too," she said.

Joe looked at Marcie, amazed at her take on things. He found it ironic that she was passing on such advice. His brother had left her at the altar years ago. Joe didn't see any signs she was dating or about to marry. Joe was afraid Marcie was a one-man woman and that man had broken her heart. He'd known her since they'd been kids. She was pretty, fun and smart as a whip. His brother had been a fool to walk away from her.

"Romantic," he said, involuntarily flicking his glaze at the fiery sunshine of the stranger's hair.

"Cynic."

"Even after Zack, you have fairy dust in your eyes."

"No, I have my faith firmly planted. Remember Pamela wasn't the only woman in the world. Open yourself up to the possibilities that surround you."

"Like Polly Maynard?" Joe asked.

Marcie burst out laughing. "Not Polly! Is she still chasing you?"

"You'd think she'd get the hint," he grumbled.

Polly had had a crush on him since high school. He'd never even dated her, but she had made it clear she'd say yes if he ever asked.

Marcie chuckled as she led Joe across the wide restaurant to the table where Gillian sat.

Gillian watched the man rise and head toward her. He'd stand out in any crowd—tall and broad shouldered, with dark hair just a bit longer than it should be. It looked rugged against his white shirt collar.

By the look on his face, he was not thrilled to be meeting her. Maybe the restaurant owner had been a bit presumptuous in thinking he'd want to show her to her new inheritance. She didn't want to be a burden on anyone, especially not a new neighbor.

And what a neighbor. He only improved as he got closer. The air seemed brighter, colors more vibrant. His long lanky build put him well over six feet. Noted since she was five ten herself. His dark hair gleamed beneath the artificial light. His tanned skin showed he spent a lot of time outdoors. And his slightly rugged build had her curious about what he might be doing in those out door hours—fishing? Rocky Point's main industry was fishing.

"Joe Kincaid, meet Gillian Parker," Marcie introduced.

"Hello. Marcie said you could show me how to get to Sophie Parker's house. It's mine now, and I don't know where it is, except somewhere out on a road called Shoreline. Sophie was my great-grandmother," she said, her words rushing through before he could say anything.

She stopped for breath. She should at least let him get a word in edgewise. Nerves shimmered as she stared into eyes that spoke volumes. *Lord, help me here. I'm such a fish out of water.*

He didn't know her, but he didn't like her. She could tell. Or was it Sophie he hadn't liked and he'd transferred those feelings to her?

"I didn't know Sophie had a great-granddaughter," he said.

She almost sighed. No one had. Except the attorney.

"That makes two of us. I was surprised when the attorney called two days ago to tell me she'd died and I was her sole beneficiary. I never even knew about her."

Surprised, then devastated to discover she'd had a living relative that she'd never known about, Gillian wished Sophie Parker had contacted her. The attorney had no trouble locating her. If he knew about her, Sophie must have also.

Why hadn't Sophie tried to contact her over the years?

When Joe didn't reply, the sudden silence increased her

nervousness. She glanced at Marcie and then took a deep breath, smiling brightly, covering her feelings of inadequacy as she had for so long. "If you're busy, maybe you can just tell me how to get to the house. Sophie's attorney gave me the key."

Stunned when she'd first learned of the legacy, Gillian was now anxious to see the house. To walk through the rooms and discover if she could learn more about this relative and perhaps uncover the facts as to why Sophie hadn't contacted her only great-grandchild while she'd been alive.

Maybe she'd be able to discover more information about her own father while she was at it. Something that would help her understand the man she hadn't seen in two decades.

"Sophie's house is next door to mine," he said, studying her as if he wasn't sure what to make of her.

She wondered if she had crumbs around her mouth or something.

"Looks like you two will be neighbors," Marcie said brightly, with an odd look at Joe. "Won't that be interesting?"

Interesting? Peculiar choice of words, Gillian thought, but her excitement grew. In only a little while, she'd see the house she now owned! She couldn't imagine owning a house in a small town in Maine. How different from an apartment in Las Vegas would that be?

Twenty minutes later, Gillian followed when Joe turned into the driveway leading to a huge, old, wood-frame two-story house. Paint peeled from the trim and the clapboard itself hadn't been painted in years. Despite a slight hint of decay, the house looked solid and substantial.

And for someone who had lived in cramped apartments all her life, it seemed palatial. Gillian felt a swell of excitement.

Situated on a bluff overlooking the cold north Atlantic, it obviously had been built for a large family. There would be more rooms than she'd know what to do with. The view from the windswept point was breathtaking. God's handiwork. She smiled in happiness. Tomorrow she'd get up to see the sunrise.

She pulled her car to a halt next to Joe's and climbed out, masking some of her excitement in front of her disapproving neighbor.

He looked at her over the top of his car.

"Are you staying long?"

Slowly Gillian smiled. "I'm staying forever," she said, the thrill of ownership making her almost giddy. *Thank You again, Heavenly Father, for this gift. Let me use it to glorify Your Name.*

He shook his head with a wry grin. "We'll see. Call if you need anything. I'm in the book. Joe Kincaid. Only one there."

Only one anywhere, she thought. She'd never met anyone quite like him. Was that unexpected interest due to being in a new town? She didn't think so. She wished she dare invite him in to show her around.

Before she could respond, he climbed back into his car and backed around, roaring for the road.

"I'm in New England. I knew it would be different," she murmured as she watched the car drive away.

She saw the car turn into a driveway about a quarter of a mile farther along the road. His house was equally large, sharing the same view of the sea. A small copse of wind-bent trees grew between them, but from what she could see at this distance, his place was in prime condition.

Slowly turning back to the silent house, she wondered what it would take to bring it back to the shape it had once known. Taking a deep breath, she stepped onto the porch and inserted the key into the lock. She wouldn't let anything spoil this moment. She was a homeowner!

No matter Joe Kincaid's doubts, she planned to make her home in Rocky Point. She'd quit her aerobics instructor position to come more than two thousand miles. The good Lord willing, she meant to stay. She had prayed long and hard before leaving. Stepping out in faith was not new to her. She knew the Lord would direct her path. She'd find a job, make friends, build a life. And feel like she belonged as she never had in Las Vegas.

By late afternoon, Gillian had changed her clothes, unpacked her suitcases in one of the barren bedrooms and explored every inch of her new home, dismayed to find it in a state of deterioration she had not anticipated. It would take a lot of work to refurbish and make comfortable.

She studied pictures on the mantel and on the buffet. All of strangers. She hadn't a clue who anyone was.

The few paintings were of sea scenes. Obviously Sophie had liked the sea.

Sometime in the next day or two, the lawyer had said, the two of them would go over her great-grandmother's estate to give her a full accounting. She hoped there was enough money to enable her do what was needed with the house. If not, she'd have to learn how to do the work herself.

Lead on, Lord. I will follow.

She opened some of the windows to get cross-ventilation and let the sea breeze blow out the musty air.

Venturing into the yard, she discovered a well-worn path leading to the bluff rising above the sea's edge. Feeling a tenuous connection to a woman she'd never met, she followed the path.

When she reached the cliff's edge, the view was amazing. The ocean stretched out forever, shades of grays and blues as far as she could see. Around the sweep of bay to the right sat the town of Rocky Point, jutting into the sea. Even from the distance, she could see the steeple of the church on the square where she'd heard the pastor's words at Sophie's service. She could see crowded docks where fishing boats bobbed.

Looking left, she saw another home or two along the bluff beyond Joe Kincaid's.

Below the cliff lay a wide beach. Narrow wooden stairs led down to the sandy shore.

Looking closer, she debated descending. It would be foolish to chance it before getting to know the area better. It would probably be the height of summer before she'd venture into the water. She'd enjoy walking along the bluff above the sea until then.

The breeze felt cool, carrying with it a tang of salt. Shivering slightly, she contrasted the weather with that of Las Vegas when she left two days ago. Not yet summer, nevertheless, it had been well into the eighties. Here she expected it was somewhere in the high fifties. With the warm sun on her black top and jeans, she wasn't cold, just cool after the hot desert of Nevada.

Sleeveless dresses and T-shirts were pretty much the extent of what she owned. First thing tomorrow, she'd pick up a sweater and some sweatshirts. Maine in April wasn't warm.

She turned to walk along the edge of the bluff, scanning her yard and that of her neighbors. A movement caught her eye and she saw a small child, standing near the copse of scrawny wind-bent trees, peering at her. Probably one of Joe Kincaid's kids, she thought.

She wondered if his wife would be more friendly? Or were all New Englanders as standoffish as he'd been? She'd heard small towns could be hard on newcomers. She'd hoped the fact her great-grandmother had been a resident all her life would ease her own transition into the community.

Waving, Gillian walked toward the child. Drawing closer she saw a little girl with short brown hair, dressed in jeans and a long sleeve top. She apparently didn't feel the chill in the air.

Gillian had spent hours with the children at her church, helping with Vacation Bible School each summer and teaching Sunday School. Based on her experience, she guessed the child was about six.

"Hi, I'm Gillian Parker. I've come to live here. Are you my neighbor?" She stopped several feet away from the child. Let her come closer when she felt comfortable.

"You're going to live in Sophie's house?" the little girl asked. Her expression was wary.

Gillian nodded, tilting her head to one side as she studied the solemn expression on the girl's face.

"Did you know Sophie?"

The child nodded.

"She was my great-grandmother, but I never knew her."

"Why not?"

"I don't know. I didn't even know she lived here. She knew about me, but she never contacted me."

She pushed away the pain. Had she not measured up to Sophie's expectations? Or had the breach with her father been passed on to his daughter?

"She was nice. I used to visit her a lot. I'm sorry she died."

"Me, too. I wish I could have known her."

"You don't look like Sophie," the little girl said after a moment's study.

"I think I look like my mother."

The child nodded. "And Sophie was old. You're not that old."

"Thank you."

Gillian glanced at her neighbor's house. "Does your mother let you come out here alone?"

The bluffs overlooking the sea were steep. She wouldn't risk a child of hers exploring and maybe falling over the edge.

"My mother's dead. She died when I was little."

Since the child seemed small to Gillian, she wondered how long ago it had happened. The matter-of-fact comment suggested it was a long time ago.

"I'm sorry to hear that. What's your name?"

"Jenny Kincaid."

"Well, Jenny Kincaid, it's getting cold out here. Want to come to my house and have something to drink? I don't know what I've got, but we can find something, I'm sure."

"No, thank you, I'm not supposed to talk to strangers."

Fine time to think of that, Gillian thought. "Well, we're hardly strangers if we're neighbors, are we? But you're right, you need to get your dad's permission to come visit. Ask him and we'll visit another time."

"You're not from Maine," Jenny said.

"No, I'm not. How can you tell?"

"You talk funny."

Gillian laughed, charmed by the child's forthrightness. "Actually, I think you talk funny. I'm from Las Vegas. It's in Nevada, a long way from here."

"That's out west."

"Right. The wild, wild west."

"Do you know any cowboys?"

Gillian nodded. "We had a nice rancher and several of his cowboys attend the church I went to. I know lots about cowboys. When you come to visit me, I'll tell you all about Nevada and horses and cowboys."

"Okay, I'll ask my dad."

Gillian watched her run back toward her house. As she headed to her own, she wondered if he'd grant permission. She'd like to make friends in town—even if she started with a small child.

And wasn't that interesting that her father was widowed. Not that she had any special interest. She'd just arrived and needed to get her own life going here. But it was with a lighter step she headed back to the house.

Entering she could feel the difference with the breeze whipping through. She quickly closed the windows, lingering on the ones on Joe's side of the house as she stared across the distance wondering what he'd thought about having her as his new neighbor.

As the afternoon turned to evening, the temperature dropped. She'd picked up a few necessities at the store before stopping for lunch, so she made herself a quick dinner. Tomorrow she'd go shopping for more groceries and cleaning supplies.

After washing her solitary dish and fork, she went to the room she suspected Sophie had used the most. It had a lived-in look. She sat in the chair by the corner windows. It was small for her and definitely worn. Beside the chair was a table with a well-used Bible. She flicked on the floor lamp and saw the light was perfect for reading. Her great-grandmother must have often sat in this chair reading her Bible.

She looked out the window, seeing her neighbor's home. What was Joe Kincaid doing now? Was he preparing dinner for Jenny? Had he given her a thought at all since they met? She'd been thinking about him a lot in the short time since lunch.

She wished she'd come across more polished and not so nervous when meeting him. There was only one time to make a good first impression. He'd definitely made a good one with her. What impression had she made?

Still gazing at his home, she began to idly daydream, weaving fantasy occasions for them to run into each other, and get to know each other better.

Chapter Two

One week later Joe Kincaid straightened from the fender he was patiently sanding and glared at the cause of the interruption.

"Come on, Joe," Tom said, "you have to know something. She's your next door neighbor. Give me something. Is she planning to stay or sell the old house?"

It appeared every person in town was trying to learn more about the new woman in Sophie's house, and they all came to him for information—merely because his house was situated next door to hers.

As if he had nothing better to do than hang around his new neighbor. Not that the thought hadn't crossed his mind a time or two. But in fact, he was a bit surprised she was still here. There was little to do in Rocky Point until the summer season started.

He tossed the spent sandpaper down on the concrete instead of at Tom and glared at the man who interrupted him. Tom Daggle was mayor of Rocky Point and should know better than to look to Joe for gossip. They'd known each other all their lives.

"I heard she comes to town each afternoon. You have a

better shot at running into her than I do." Joe said. She hadn't been down the street his auto restoration shop was on or he'd have noticed.

"Now, now, Joe. No need to get huffy. I thought since you're living next door to her, you would at least have been neighborly enough to have asked her to dinner or something."

"Hunt her up next time she comes to town and invite her yourself," Joe said.

"She appears to be getting acquainted with every shop owner in town. But she's not talking much about herself and so far no one knows much about her. Except she's planning some renovation at Sophie's. She spent the longest time in Hanson's furniture store," Tom said.

"Then check with Hanson."

Joe had seen Gillian once or twice at a distance. He'd thought she was just aimlessly wandering around.

"Surely you've spoken with her in a neighborly fashion, learned a bit more about her—where's she from, what her plans are. That would be the neighborly thing to do," Tom persisted.

"Nope." Joe eyed the 1930 Stutz Bearcat he was restoring. The surface was almost ready for painting. The engine already purred like a kitten. He wanted to continue working, not fend off questions about a woman he didn't know.

Life in Rocky Point would be too dull for someone like her. He knew the type. He'd *lived* with the type for four years.

"Aren't you even interested?" Tom asked.

"Nope. Look, Tom, if you want to know about her, talk to her the next time you see her. Or invite her to dinner. I've got work to do."

Tom glanced around. The three men who worked for Joe were busy at their respective tasks. The huge warehouse held five vintage cars in various stages of restoration. The large double doors at one end stood wide, to allow the April breeze to keep the temperatures down, despite welding equipment and acetylene torches.

"Heard you fired Ben Ostler."

"Yeah, he came to work drunk one time too many."

Joe cast a glance at his crew—good men all. And they each had a passion for restoring classic cars. Even Ben, when he didn't drink to excess. He'd hated to let the man go. He'd given him many chances to straighten out. But the safety of Joe's other workers came first.

"Too bad. His wife just had a new baby," Tom commented.

"And your point is?"

"Nothing. Just too bad."

"Yeah, well it's too bad he couldn't keep the bottle corked. Drunks and cars don't go together."

"Anyway, about Sophie's granddaughter—"

"Great-granddaughter. And her name's Gillian," Joe said.

Tom's sighed in exasperation. "I can't invite her to dinner. Penny would have a fit."

For a moment Joe almost smiled. "I expect so," he concurred, thinking of Tom's wife, who had been slim once upon a time when they'd all been in high school, but who was now a full-figured woman. No way would Rocky Point's women want to compare themselves with Gillian.

Except for Marcie—she wouldn't care. Twice over the last week she'd asked after Gillian when he stopped in for a quick cup of coffee, expressing disappointment that Gillian hadn't come back to the café.

Even Jenny seemed fascinated by the woman. She'd mentioned meeting her that first night. Chatted all through dinner. She'd said something about going to visit, but he'd told her not to make a bother of herself. Sometimes she stood at the window in the kitchen and stared at Sophie's house. Gillian's house, he corrected himself. He knew his daughter grieved for Sophie.

"Consider it your civic duty," Tom said.

"Go on, Tom. I have work to do even if you don't," Joe said easily, ignoring his irritation. He picked up a wad of fine steel wool. "Ask her yourself, send your secretary or find another patsy. If you want to know Gillian Parker's plans, I'd say wait a little longer. When she tires of the slow pace here, she'll be gone, and she'll put the house on the market."

"You don't think she'll stay?" Tom looked surprised at that.

"She's not from around here. She's sure to have a place with friends and family around. And a lot more going on than we have in Rocky Point."

"Rocky Point is a great place to live," Tom said.

Joe nodded, hoping Tom wasn't going to start in on his civic pride speech. He began to rub the fine steel wool against the fender.

"I know the spiel, Tom. Rocky Point is great for raising a family. Gillian Parker's a Las Vegas showgirl. She'll never stay."

"Las Vegas showgirl? How'd you know that? Thought you said you haven't talked to her."

"Jenny told me. She saw her out walking one day and spoke with her a couple of minutes." Joe could have bitten his tongue. He hadn't wanted to continue their conversation. He'd had enough.

When the mayor finally left, Joe resumed smoothing the replaced fender in preparation for the paint. The task left him free to think. Often this was the best time to talk with the Lord. No one interrupted, and the soothing repetition of the work gave him freedom for prayer.

Despite his words, he'd like to know what Gillian's plans were. He'd seen her in the distance a couple of times, walking along the bluff. She seemed fascinated by the sea.

He'd made no overtures. No attempts to speak with her. Yet if he admitted it to himself, he was as fascinated by her as his daughter was. She wore old jeans and baggy shirts. Her hair was often tied back, as if to keep it out of her face.

He'd have liked to know her impressions of the house, of the town. Was she as captivated by the sea as it seemed by her daily walks along the bluff? Coming from the Nevada desert, she must find Rocky Point completely different. In a good way?

He'd been tempted, but resisted going out to meet her. He hadn't made any efforts to get to know her. He wasn't sure how to talk to her without giving an impression he was interested. So rather than give rise to speculation, he stayed away.

The fact she kept to herself surprised him. Sophie had no television, so Gillian couldn't be spending time watching TV.

And he suspected Sophie's taste in literature would not appeal.

She looked the part of a showgirl, he'd thought the instant Jenny had told him where she hailed from. All flash and long legs and glorious golden-red hair.

Disapproving of that lifestyle, he hadn't encouraged Jenny to pursue a friendship. She seemed content with his casual remarks. He didn't want to give rise to any arguments with her if he could help it. His little girl was still fragile from Sophie's death.

In the meantime, he was a responsible father. A pillar in the community, as Marcie had often said. Rocky Point suited him fine.

Not for him the dreams of greatness, bright lights or a fast-paced lifestyle. He had built a solid reputation for reliability and outstanding work over the last few years with his restorations of vintage cars. The work might not be glamorous, but he liked it. It paid well and gave him a strong sense of connection with the past.

And the business also provided the livelihood of four other men. Until Ben had caused a problem. He had enough work coming in to begin to look for another employee.

Joe and Jenny lived in his family's home. He was raising his daughter with old-fashioned values. He'd had enough of people who wanted to walk on the wild side—like his wife Pamela or his brother, Zack.

Where had it gotten them? His brother never came home,

and his wife was in a grave six feet deep.

Rocky Point wasn't for everyone—especially a Las Vegas showgirl.

For some reason, Marcie's comments after the funeral popped into his mind. She thought he should find another wife. He'd sworn off the idea after Pamela died while leaving him.

There was no one in town who interested him—especially Polly.

He'd tried marriage. It hadn't worked out. End of story.

The next afternoon Joe took a break from work to run to the supermarket to pick up some cold drinks for the shop. He usually included soft drinks in his normal grocery shopping, but the warmer weather had the men going through sodas faster than normal.

His cart loaded up, he rounded a corner and stopped. Gillian stood in the middle of the aisle looking at the ingredients for baking. He hesitated for only a second, then pushed on.

"Hello," he said.

She looked up and smiled.

Joe felt like he'd been slugged with a two by four. That smile should be registered as a lethal weapon. He felt soft and squishy inside.

Get a grip he admonished himself.

"Hi, neighbor." She looked at the cart full of soft drinks and widened her eyes. "My, you do like sodas."

"It's for the guys at work. Shopping?"

A dumb comment if ever he heard it. What else would she be doing in a grocery store.

"I came for some fresh veggies but thought I might like to make brownies or cookies or something." She began looking at the items on the shelves again.

"I like cookies myself," he said.

She looked back at him, that smile still on her face. "Duly noted. If I do bake cookies, I'll send some your way. Save me eating them all."

"Jenny would like them, too," he said, already worried he'd come on too strong.

He hoped she didn't think he was suggesting she make him cookies.

"All kids like cookies." Her eyes seemed to light up. "I guess even adults who never quite grew up like cookies, too."

He could stare at her smiling face for hours. And for a moment forgot the supermarket and just enjoyed her smile.

When Mrs. Hatton, a long-time member of his church rounded the corner and almost bumped into him, the spell was broken.

"You're blocking the aisle, Joe," she complained.

"Sorry. Gotta go."

He maneuvered his cart around Gillian's and walked away, already forgetting what he had wanted on that aisle.

"Joe?" she called after him.

He looked back, saw the speculative look of Mrs. Hatton. "Yeah?"

"Chocolate chip cookies okay?"

"My favorites."

He nodded to both women and headed toward checkout. So if she made cookies, she'd have to bring them over. And he could ask her in to share them. Not that he'd been hinting. Or had he? He wondered if she'd bring them today. Maybe he'd take off work early and make sure the house was straight.

Joe got home from work in time to meet the school bus. Most days Jenny came to the shop directly from school, but he'd cut out early today and left a message for her at the school. Jenny didn't hop off the bus with her usual enthusiasm. Instead, she dragged down the driveway, looking as if the weight of the world sat on her shoulders.

"Tough day?" he asked from his seat on the top step to the porch when she reached him. His heart expanded with love. He adored his little girl. She was the joy of his life. He said a quick prayer for God to always watch over her and keep her safe. And another prayer of thanksgiving that she'd been spared in the crash that had taken her mother's life.

"Melissa's getting a pony. She's taking riding lessons and is going to learn to compete in horse shows. Can I have a horse? Can I learn to ride?" she asked, a hint of hope in her voice.

"Maybe when you're older," he said, scooping her up and hugging her close. The mere thought of a runaway horse throwing Jenny sent chills down his spine. She was too young to think of horses or a bicycle that could careen out in front of a car or a skateboard that could run away with her.

"You're always saying that," she said, frowning and pushing to be set down. "I'm never going to get to do anything!"

She ran into the house. Ten seconds later Joe heard the slam of her bedroom door.

He'd blown it—again. Half the time he didn't know if what he was doing was right for Jenny, restricting her activities. But he was afraid to risk his child's safety. He'd almost lost her once. After surviving those dark days in the hospital, so afraid she wouldn't recover, there was no way he was willing to risk her safety.

Sighing, he entered the house and wondered how to give her a glimpse of excitement while keeping her safe.

He wished his parents were alive to help. But they had died in a freak boating accident before he married Pamela. Parenting should be a two-person job. If only—

Gillian once again had opened all the windows and relished the cool air blowing through the house. In the week since she'd arrived, the changes to her home were nothing short of remarkable.

Months of accumulated dust had vanished. Much of the furniture had been revived with judicious polishing and cleaning.

Granted, the draperies and curtains were worn and frayed, but with the grime gone from the windows, she loved the view. Taking down the dirty, heavy coverings had opened all the rooms to the brightness and splendor of the setting. There were no trees close, so she had sun all day long. She wasn't sure if she would put up any curtains. She liked the big, picture-perfect view she had from every window: the sea on one side, a glimpse of Rocky Point from another room and the green land rolling west of the front of the house.

Maybe curtains in the bedroom—for privacy. But that room faced the sea. A boat on the water would need a powerful telescope to see into her room. Not that she'd noticed any boats lurking around for the chance.

She'd spent every afternoon becoming more familiar with Rocky Point. She loved the small town. The stores were all distinctive and individual. No big chains in Rocky Point.

The clerks and shopkeepers were friendly and helpful. When she'd told the woman who owned the fabric store some of her ideas about decorating, she'd immediately given her the name of a seamstress who did great work at low cost—for curtains and perhaps slipcovers.

She'd bought the ingredients for chocolate-chip cookies and had begun to make the dough. It was fun to bake for someone else. She smiled remembering the few moments at the grocery store. She wondered if Joe would have said anything further if the older woman hadn't come into their aisle.

She glanced out the back window at the sea. She loved seeing it in all the different colors. Between her and the water, however, was the large pile of trash she'd been accumulating as she had cleared the heavy, dirty window coverings from each room. The pile also had broken furniture, old newspapers and magazines dating from before she'd been born and it looked like the trash heap it was. She needed to call someone to haul it away.

Maybe Joe could suggest who to call. She'd ask when she took over the cookies.

Stirring the batter, she caught a glimpse of Jenny heading her way. In a moment she heard the familiar knock at the back door. She enjoyed the visits of her young neighbor. She wished Jenny would bring her father some time.

"Come on in, the door's open."

"I know," Jenny said, stepping politely inside the huge family-style kitchen. "You always leave it unlocked. But it's polite to knock. Sophie said so. She left the door unlocked, too."

"It's safe, right?" Gillian asked, already getting down another cup.

Jenny liked hot chocolate with lots of marshmallows. Apparently so had Sophie. The fixings had been easy to find.

"Surely such a small town doesn't have a criminal element."

Jenny walked to the stove, tilted her head as if considering what Gillian had said. "Does that mean bad guys?"

"Right."

"No, we don't have any. Does Las Vegas?"

Gillian nodded, grinning at Jenny. "You could say that. Did you finish your homework already?"

"I didn't do it. And I left before Daddy could take me to the shop. I'm mad at him, you know." She plopped on one of the chairs and kicked her heels against the crosspiece. "He said I can't have a pony."

"Oh. Well, that would make me angry, too. I always wanted a pony when I was little."

Gillian prepared the hot beverages. "I never got one either," she confided.

"So maybe you could buy a pony now," Jenny said practically. "And if you do, you could let me ride it."

"I don't think I'm up to horse ownership just yet. I still have lots to do around here."

She needed to confer with the attorney and see about finding a job. She'd put off both tasks until she'd decided for sure to remain in Rocky Point.

"I don't get to do anything!" Jenny complained. "Every time I ask Daddy about something, he says maybe when I'm older. Then I'll be grown up and won't want a bike."

"Maybe he means just a little older, not when you're grown up. Do you want a bike?" Gillian thought they'd been talking about ponies.

Jenny nodded enthusiastically. "All of the girls in my class have one, and they get together after school and go riding down to the ice cream store or Auntie Marcie's and then out to the park and have fun. I'm stuck at Daddy's old shop every afternoon."

"Where is your father's store?" Gillian asked, diverted.

She could picture Joe Kincaid as a hardware store owner or maybe something to do with heavy farm equipment, but not much else. The suit and tie he'd worn at the funeral hadn't seemed like him somehow. He looked too active to be content to sit behind a desk all day. She was going to be majorly disappointed if he sold furniture or something.

Jenny laughed. "He doesn't have a store—he has a *shop!* He fixes cars."

"Oh, so he's a mechanic?" That occupation better fit the image she carried with her ever since their initial meeting. She'd seen him once or twice when on her walks, but he'd made no effort to close the distance and neither had she. Their brief encounter at the store hadn't been conducive to exchanging information—except that he liked chocolate chip cookies.

"I don't know. The cars are old. Sometimes I sit in them before they're finished and pretend I'm driving. Then Daddy always takes each of us for a ride when the car is ready to be sent back to its owner."

"Are there more kids at home?" Gillian looked at Jenny. The couple of times the child had stopped by to visit this week she had not mentioned any brothers or sisters. Gillian had not questioned the child, respecting the privacy of her neighbors. But that didn't help her curiosity. After the friendly meeting at the store, she wanted to know even more about her neighbor.

"What home?"

"Yours."

"Nope. I'm an only. Auntie Marcie says my dad should get married and have a houseful of kids. How many would that be?"

"Lots. Who does he give rides to?"

"The other guys what work in the shop. It's near the docks. They have fire guns and everything. It's neat."

"I'd like to see it sometime," Gillian said, wondering what fire guns were. Talking with Jenny brightened her day. She never knew what the child would say next. She reminded her of the six-year-olds she'd taught Sunday School for the last few years. She missed her class and the funny things the children said.

Jenny shrugged, dipping her spoon into the melted marshmallow mess floating on her hot chocolate and licking it delightedly. "This is good. We hardly ever—"

Suddenly Gillian held up a finger, straining to listen. Had she heard Jenny's name called?

Only silence.

"I thought I heard something," Gillian said. She narrowed her gaze at the child. "Does your daddy know you're over here?"

Jenny shook her head. "I just left. I told you, I'm mad at him."

"Well mad or not, you need to let him know—" She heard the sound of running, and then a pounding on her screen door.

"Gillian!"

She rose and hurried to the door in response to the strain in his voice. Joe Kincaid stood there, looking twice as big as she remembered—and twice as handsome—in worn jeans and a flannel shirt with the sleeves rolled back.

And worried to death.

"Jenny's here," she said quickly, opening the door.

"Thank You, God!" He crushed a cloth doll in one hand, closing his eyes briefly. "I found this near the top of the bluff—by the stairs. For a moment I thought she'd gone down to the beach even though she knows she shouldn't—" He stepped inside and immediately spotted his daughter.

"What's going on?" The anxiety faded from his voice.

Suspicion replaced it.

"Hi, Daddy," Jenny said, her eyes on her cup, her spoon already dipping into the melted marshmallow again.

"I just learned you didn't know she was here," Gillian explained, feeling oddly guilty. She'd nothing to feel guilty about. She hadn't lured Jenny here. The child had come of her own free will, assuring her that Joe didn't mind.

He glanced at her, his eyes dark and unfathomable, then looked away. "Why is she here?"

"She came to visit. We're having hot chocolate. Want some?"

He looked at Jenny. "I told you not to bother the new neighbor."

She looked up at that. "I'm not bothering you, am I, Gillian?"

"Not at all. I enjoy your company."

The sunny smile seemed to anger her father. He shook his head. "That's not what I meant."

"What *did* you mean?" Gillian asked.

He avoided eye contact. Was her face smeared with dirt? Was her hair a wild tangled mess? She wished she had a mirror nearby to check. Had she imagined their meeting at the store. He didn't seem as friendly at the moment.

"I meant she wasn't to come over," he said, speaking to Jenny.

"Visiting isn't bothering, Daddy," Jenny said, slurping her chocolate noisily. "Besides, visiting Gillian is educational. She's telling me all about Las Vegas."

"Great." At that he did look at Gillian. "The last thing I

want is my daughter to get any ideas about the glamorous life on the Strip. Is that clear? I don't want her head filled with nonsense or fanciful dreams that will only bring discontent and unhappiness. In the future, she'll stay in our yard!" He nailed Jenny with a look. "Is that clear, young lady?"

Gillian almost felt as if she should salute but wisely said nothing. She was a bit taken aback that he thought she would corrupt a seven-year-old with wild tales of the infamous Las Vegas Strip, even if she knew any.

In less than a minute, man and child were gone.

"I guess that's perfectly clear," she said slowly, as the sound of receding footsteps grew faint. "I'm not good enough for your daughter."

The hurt pierced unexpectedly. No one had ever outright told her she wasn't suitable before. Though it was a familiar feeling. Her father had deserted her when she'd been a young child. And now she discovered her great-grandmother had never tried to contact her during her lifetime.

Before she could deal with the churning emotions that arose, the phone rang.

"Hello?" It was her first call on the house phone. She knew no one in town, except her grumpy neighbor, and she sure didn't expect him to be calling. He'd made that perfectly clear.

"Miss Parker? Julian Greene here, Sophie's attorney."

"Yes, Mr. Greene. I know I should have called for an appointment, but I've been busy."

She really did need to go see the man to get the estate cleared up. She could use some funds before long—if there were any. But from the condition of the house, she suspected money had been very tight for her great-grandmother.

He cleared his throat. "Actually, it is important that we meet fairly quickly. Something has come up that requires immediate attention."

"Oh?"

"Sophie's grandson has just shown up, claiming her estate."

"Sophie's grandson? *My father?*"

"That's right. He claims he's the rightful heir and plans to challenge the will."

Gillian gripped the receiver tightly as the room seemed to spin. Slowly she leaned against the wall and sank to the floor.

"My father? My father's in town?" She hadn't seen the man since she was eight. "How can that be?"

Julian Greene cleared his throat. "Actually, he arrived this afternoon. He's in my office now, and, er, is anxious to get things settled."

"Tell her not to touch a thing." A masculine voice came faintly across the line.

Gillian could scarcely breathe. Her father. The man who had run out on her mother and her, and who had never made any attempt to contact them since.

Who was now trying to take her inheritance!

"I thought you said Sophie had you write her will."

"Ah, so she did. Several years ago, in fact. But your father claims he has a more recent will. It apparently supersedes the one I wrote for her."

Oh, Lord, help me through this. Show me Your will, please.

Anger built. She felt as if her father had been in the wings, waiting to jump out and snatch the dream from her hand. How could he!

"I'll be in tomorrow, Mr. Greene. We can hash it out then. But until it's settled one way or another, I'm staying right here!"

She surprised herself with her stand. But she also had no where else to go and wanted to remain, if only for a short time, in the house where her great-grandmother meant for her to stay.

She clutched the receiver to her chest, gripping it so tightly her fingers ached. She needed to stand to reach the phone base to hang up. But she couldn't listen to another word. Pressing it against her shirt, she muffled the words that were ending her dream.

Then she took a deep breath. *Lord, Thy will be done. Show me the path You have for me*, she prayed silently. She knew so little about the man who had fathered her. Her mother had loved him, but he hadn't stayed long enough for Gillian to know him. Always chasing after the quick buck, her mother had said. The fondness and regret in her tone had told Gillian she'd loved him in spite of his ways.

Taking another deep breath, Gillian tried to bring some order into the chaos of her thoughts. She went through the motions of baking the cookies, the happiness she'd experienced when making the dough evaporated with what had happened since she started. She probably wouldn't be taking any cookies to Joe and Jenny.

Now she wasn't sure she wanted any herself.

Looking around the room, she didn't see the scarred table or the faded linoleum. She saw instead the bright paint she'd planned to use, the sunny yellow that would brighten the kitchen walls and bring a warmth to the room, even on dreary, gray winter days. She'd planned to paint the dark cupboards white and replace serviceable knobs with fanciful ones. Grow herbs in the window, bake cookies that would fill the house with wonderful fragrances.

Only the room might not be hers to do with as she pleased anymore.

Could the house really belong to her father?

She could scarcely stand against the wave of bitter disappointment.

Moving slowly, she went into the living room and sank down on the corner chair. Gazing out of the window at the waning day, she opened her heart in prayer.

Chapter Three

Joe Kincaid glanced at the clock. Almost one in the morning. He stretched out on his bed, wishing things could go back the way they'd been two weeks ago—before Sophie had a stroke and fallen down those stairs. Before she'd died.

Everything had been easier then. Jenny went to school and came home to do her homework. She didn't complain she couldn't do things the other girls in her class did or talk endlessly about a pretty neighbor. And he didn't lie awake at night thinking about her.

He'd been totally rude when he found Jenny at Gillian's. He'd have to go apologize. He'd been frantic—not that how he'd felt was a reason for lashing out. But suddenly he'd seen what Pamela had yearned for in Gillian—pretty, from a fast-pace lifestyle. And he'd seen his daughter taken with her. Was that what rankled the most? That Gillian had such an easy way with her Jenny had already been captivated?

He'd apologize and maybe offer to take her to lunch or something to make up for his behavior. He'd have to explain, too.

He stared into the darkness trying to go over the things he needed to do the next day. It was Saturday, and he'd promised Jenny they'd do something special together. But his thoughts kept sliding toward the house next door. If he apologized early, maybe she could join them. Jenny would like that.

Her kitchen gleamed when he'd retrieved Jenny that afternoon. And had smelled delicious with cookies baking. In contrast, Gillian had looked a bit bedraggled. Her flame-colored hair had drawn his attention like a candle drew a moth. But the faded jeans and wrinkled top belied the flash and glamour. There'd been a smudge of something on the edge of her jaw and no makeup.

She'd offered to make cookies. Was that a first step in friendship? He wished she'd come to borrow something or waved and come to meet him when he'd seen her on her walks.

But maybe she was shy. A stranger in town who knew no one and who obviously came from a different background.

The thought intrigued him. She looked too confident and pretty to be shy, but maybe.

Who was he trying to convince?

She hadn't shown a hint of interest in him. And she'd had plenty of time to do so since she moved in. She could have pumped Jenny about his favorite foods, then brought over a hot dish. But she'd done nothing like that.

He rose from his bed and pulled on a pair of jeans. Sleep proved too elusive. He might as well get some paperwork done in the office. Sooner or later he'd be tired enough to crash no matter what.

He glanced out the window, paused. Was that a light? A

flickering light?

He went to the window and raised the lower half, peering into the darkness. There.

His heart sank. It looked like a fire at Sophie's place.

Joe snatched up his phone and dialed 911. Thrusting his feet into shoes as he gave the information to Natalie Benson, the emergency operator, he tossed the phone down as soon as he was finished and grabbed a shirt, already running.

Jumping into the truck, he gunned the engine and barreled across the field between the two houses. The fire was growing. It was at the back of the house. *Please Lord, guard Gillian. Keep her safe. Let me be in time.*

The place was a tinderbox—it'd go up in a flash. As he drew closer, he realized the trash Gillian had piled up behind the house was ablaze, not the house itself.

Still, the old dried wooden structure wouldn't take much to ignite if the flames from the pile grew.

He leaned on the car horn. Was she awake? Did she know there was a fire about to incinerate her home?

Slamming the truck to a stop near the fire, he leaped out just as a window upstairs opened.

"What—oh, no!" Gillian appeared briefly, then vanished.

Joe didn't wait to see more. She was awake, and she could get out safely. He ran to the side of the house, looking for a hose, something to stop the growth of the flames, which seemed to be greedily consuming the pile so near the old structure.

He found nothing. But it was still too early for gardening and had been before Sophie's death. No need to have the hose in the yard.

The back door flew open and Gillian ran out, carrying a pot of water. She tossed it ineffectively at the fire and turned back.

"We need more than that," Joe called, rounding the corner of the house. "Where's a hose?"

"I don't know. I just moved here. Did you call the fire department?"

In the dancing light, she looked scared to death, standing in front of him in flannel pajamas.

"Yes, get away from the house. It could go up any moment."

"No!" She ran back inside and was back in a moment with another pot of water, which she threw futilely on the growing conflagration. "I'm not losing this house!"

The heat was intense and growing. The breeze from the ocean bent the blaze toward the old clapboard. The roar increased as more and more of the debris exploded into flame.

Joe ran across the yard to the small shed and threw open the door. A hose was coiled neatly on a rack. He grabbed it and two shovels and ran back, blood pounding in his veins. Where was the fire truck? How long would it take for the volunteers to get here?

The next few minutes were a blur. He ordered Gillian to connect the hose, while he tried to build a firebreak trench between the house and fire. The heat almost seared his skin, but if they were to save the house they needed to keep the fire away.

She came running back, water streaming from the hose.

Aiming it at the fire, she tried to get closer, but he could tell the intensity of the heat was too much.

"Spray the house," he yelled, turning away to give himself some respite from the heat. "We aren't going to put the fire out with that hose, so let's see if we can get the house wet enough to keep from catching."

She adjusted the spray to a finer mist and turned it on him first. The shock of cold water caused him to catch his breath, but the instant relief from the fire's heat was wonderful.

She turned the nozzle toward the house, spraying as high as she could and letting the water trail down the side of the old structure.

Joe heard the sirens in the distance.

Gillian drew closer, trying to extend the spray across as large an area as she could.

Just then there was an explosive shift in the pile. A flaming piece of wood flew out, bounced against the house and ricocheted toward her. Joe leaped in front of her and caught the burning chair leg. He yelled, tossing it away, his hands already feeling the searing pain.

She spun him around, the water soaking his legs.

"Let me see!"

He held out his hands, already blistering and raw red.

Slowly she edged them near the water until the edge of the fine mist covered them. He jerked back in agony.

Sirens screaming, lights flashing, Rocky Point's fire engine lumbered into the yard. In seconds water was pumping, men scrambling to aim their hose at the flames and at the house, fighting the fire, doing their best to save the old structure.

The sheriff pulled in behind the truck. Following him was the county ambulance.

Gillian dropped her hose and took Joe's arm, pulling him away.

"Let the professionals take care of the rest. You need to have someone see to those burns. Oh, Joe, I'm so sorry—your poor hands!"

As they walked to the ambulance, the scene became surreal, red and blue lights rotated, mingling with the wavering yellow of the flame. Shouts and commands combined with the static voices of radios as men moved to contain the blaze before it could do more damage.

"This is all I can do here, Joe," the EMT said a few minutes later, after covering Joe's burns. "You'll have to see Doc Martin. We'll transport you. Anyone else need medical assistance?"

Gillian turned back to the scene. The firefighters had contained the blaze, and it was already diminished. Her house looked safe.

"I don't think so," she said.

"I'll come in first thing tomorrow," Joe said. "I can't leave Jenny."

"I'll go watch her. You get your hands taken care of."

She looked up at him. The erratic light shone on her cheeks, making her eyes look dark and mysterious. Even in the darkness, her hair shone like a flame.

"Thank you, Joe. You saved my life and my home. You're a hero."

He almost laughed. "Not on your life, showgirl. You'd

have done what you could to save someone who was in danger, right?"

She looked at him oddly. "I'm not a showgirl," she said. "Not everyone who lives in Las Vegas works at casinos. Is that what you thought?"

He took a deep breath but his hands hurt so bad now he wasn't sure he could think straight.

"I'll watch Jenny. If they keep you at the hospital, we'll come in the morning," she said.

"They won't keep me," he vowed, reluctantly agreeing to seek medical treatment. He hated leaving his daughter with a stranger, but he didn't have any choice. "The back door is probably standing wide open. She should sleep through until morning."

"Unless she heard the sirens and all. If so, I'll reassure her," Gillian said.

"Thanks."

She smiled at him.

"Ready?" the EMT asked.

He nodded and stepped into the ambulance. He hoped Doc Martin had some miracle cure, because his hands burned like crazy.

As they pulled away, he gave a brief prayer of thanks that God had kept them safe and had saved Gillian's house.

After ducking back into her house to get dressed, she headed for Joe's house. She hoped Jenny had slept through all the commotion or she'd probably be terrified with her father gone and all the activity here.

Stepping outside, Gillian was pleased to see the fire was

completely out. Only a soggy smoldering mess of ash and partially burned debris remained. The firefighters continued pouring on water.

"Gillian Parker?" The sheriff ambled over, glancing at the remains of the fire. The fire chief was walking around, studying it.

"Yes."

"Sheriff Johnston. Mind if I ask you a few questions?"

"Not at all, but could we do it at Joe's house? He was injured and taken to the hospital, and I said I'd go watch Jenny for him."

"Fine with me." He turned to call to the fire chief, "Gordon, I'm taking Miss Parker over to Joe's place. I'll meet up with you back in town." Turning back to Gillian, he nodded toward his car. "We can drive."

Five minutes later Gillian came downstairs and reentered Joe's kitchen. The sheriff sat at the small table in a breakfast nook as if he had done so many times before.

"Jenny asleep?" he asked when she entered.

"Sound asleep. I would have thought she'd have heard the sirens, if nothing else."

The sheriff smiled. "Kids can sleep through anything."

"So I see," Gillian said, sitting slowly in the chair opposite.

"Know how the fire started?" he asked, pulling out a small notebook.

She shook her head. "I have no idea."

"When did you discover it?"

She shook her head again. "Actually Joe did, because the first thing I knew I woke up because someone was blowing a car horn. I looked out the window to see who it was and saw the fire. Did piling all that old stuff cause a spontaneous combustion?"

"Don't know what caused it yet. But that's unlikely. Why did you have such a pile there to begin with?"

Gillian explained her cleaning and clearing tactics over the past week, ending with her intent to call someone to haul the debris away once she was finished.

The sheriff asked a few more questions, took a few more notes and then thanked her. He asked if she'd be okay and left when she assured him she was fine.

Gillian watched the car drive away. She couldn't see her house very well from the back door, but its dark outline was visible. Her home was safe. She offering up a prayer to the Lord for her safety and the help of her neighbor. *Please, Father God, let Joe's injuries be slight and heal them quickly. He did it for me. And thank You for letting him see the fire before it burned the house.*

Threatened twice in one day—first by her father's arrival, now by a fire. Was that house jinxed? Maybe she wasn't supposed to have it after all. *Show me the path You want me to take, Lord.*

Closing the door, she wandered around the first floor, switching on lights, idly looking around Joe Kincaid's home— sturdy furnishings, seascapes on the walls, childish drawings on the refrigerator, dolls and crayons everywhere. Sinking into a comfortable sofa in a well-used living room, she drew her legs up and lay back against the soft, welcoming cushions. Before long, the tension began to drain. She didn't even realize when she fell asleep.

"I appreciate this, Marcie," Joe said as she turned into his driveway.

"So you've said five times," she replied in amusement. "Honestly, I'm glad to do it. Your call in the middle of the night scared me. Asking for a ride home was nothing after that."

"I could have waited for the sheriff's deputy to bring me back instead of having you get up."

"Hey, it's not that long until dawn. I get up early. You know that."

"Yeah."

He knew she liked to be at the restaurant well before it opened at seven. But getting up early wasn't the same thing as being woken at 4:00 a.m. to drive him home from the doctor's.

"Besides, I wanted to make sure you're okay," she said.

"I will be, in a few weeks. What I'm going to do in the meantime, I'm not sure. I have delivery dates to meet, chores around the house, Jenny to take care of."

"Maybe she'd like to come spend some time with me. And you've got good men working for you. What you can't deliver, you can't. Clients will understand."

He frowned staring at his house. "Why are all the lights on?"

"We'll soon find out."

Marcie stopped near the back door and hardly had the engine turned off before he was running to the back door. Joe gasped in pain as he wrenched open the door without thinking. His hands hurt! The doctor had told him even with the pain meds it would take a while for the pain to subside.

She followed quickly, hoping the lights didn't mean there was anything wrong. Stepping inside, she glanced around and headed for the front of the house. Nothing seemed out of place.

Joe was coming slowly down the stairs. Seeing her, he said, "Jenny's sound asleep. I didn't see Gillian."

"I'm not upstairs," Gillian said from the living room.

She sat up and looked at them over the back of the sofa. "I checked on Jenny when I first got here. She was fine. I didn't mean to fall asleep. Are you all right?"

Spotting his bandaged hands, she winced and quickly rose, crossing to the bottom of the stairs.

"You're not, are you?" she said, frowning at the sight of his hands.

"I'll be right as rain in a few weeks," Joe said.

"Gillian, how're you holding up?" Marcie asked. "Joe told me about the fire. What caused it, do you know?"

Gillian shook her head. "The sheriff asked, too. I thought maybe spontaneous combustion. But he says likely not." She eyed Joe's hands then met his gaze steadily. "Thank you again. I owe you."

"No, you don't."

"For?" Marcie asked.

Gillian quickly explained how Joe burned his hands. "Didn't he tell you?"

Marcie shook her head, her gaze on Joe. "Only that he'd been injured fighting the fire. I didn't know he'd been the one to first see it. Interesting."

"Interesting, nothing. Just lucky." He swayed a bit. "If you ladies will excuse me, I think I'll head for bed."

"Sure thing. Want me to stay for Jenny?" Marcie asked.

"I can do that," Gillian said swiftly. "I'll make breakfast. You sleep in as long as you can."

"I see you're in good hands," Marcie said. "Go upstairs. We'll both be here in case Jenny wakes."

"There's no need to stay. Jenny and I manage in the morning," he said stiffly.

Gillian shrugged. "I doubt it. Take advantage of help when it comes. If you don't let us stay, you deny us the chance to help."

"I don't need you to stay."

"Men can be so grumpy when ill," Marcie said. "Scoot, Joe. Gillian and I will watch over Jenny."

He frowned. "I'm not *that* tired."

Gillian's eyes narrowed. "You're swaying on your feet. If they haven't already, the pain pills will start to work soon. You'll be out like a light."

He shrugged.

Hands on her hips, she studied him. "I wish I had a Bible verse for just this occasion. How about Proverbs 16:18?"

Joe narrowed his eyes. His gaze met hers. The amusement dancing in her blue eyes fired up that interest he hadn't had before. Which Bible verse was that?

He turned and climbed the stairs, never letting his posture waver, though he was dead tired and his hands hurt. His movements slowed until he felt he was slogging through cold molasses. But before he gave in to the desire to fall into bed, he picked up his Bible with clumsy bandaged fingers and turned to Proverbs.

Pride goeth before destruction.

She was right—he felt as if he'd fall on his face. Closing the book, he shed his shoes and jeans and crawled beneath the covers. But sleep didn't come right away. His hands hurt. And his conscience . He still needed to apologize.

"Did you know he thought I was a showgirl from Vegas?" Gillian asked, following Marcie into the living room.

"Did he?" She plopped on the sofa and rested her head against the high-back cushions. "I'm so tired. I'm glad he called me to get him from the hospital, but another couple hours of sleep would have been welcomed."

"Do I look like a Las Vegas showgirl," Gillian persisted.

Marcia opened her eyes and looked at her and shrugged. "Probably, or maybe because you have a dancer's body and move so gracefully," Marcie said.

"Can't anyone look beyond the obvious?" she asked in disgust. "Did you think that, too?" Gillian plopped down on the sofa. She crossed her arms across her chest and glared at Marcie.

"You're not a dancer?" Marcie said.

"I have taught dance, but my primary job's been as an aerobics instructor at a gym. I work with some of the showgirls but feel it's a way to witness for Jesus. The majority of the women who come to the gym are working women, mothers or young singles. They do not wear the scanty costumes the dancers on the Strip do." She leaned back and frowned. "Is that what everyone in town thinks?"

"I have no idea what everyone in town thinks," Marcie said.

She studied Gillian for a moment and sighed. "Even in the middle of the night, your gorgeous."

Gillian looked at Marcie. After a moment, she shrugged. "I can't take credit for that. My Heavenly Father created me to look just like this. He had his reasons, I'm sure, but sometimes it's more a liability than asset in the secular world. Away from Las Vegas, I thought things might be different. Tell me, is the church where the services for Sophie were held a good one? I missed last Sunday, but I'd like to go this week."

"My dad has been going to Trinity Church since before I was born. Sophie always attended there, too. Pastor John and his wife are real sweethearts."

"I met them at the funeral. They came to call earlier in the week, so I wanted to try the church. I belong to a great church in Vegas, but I want to put down roots here." If she got the chance.

Julian Greene had agreed to meet with her first thing Saturday. It wasn't enough that the house almost burned to the ground. Now she had to face a battle to save it on another front.

"I think I'll check Jenny one more time," she said, jumping up. The child remained fast asleep when she peeped into her room. She swiped a couple of blankets from the linen closet near the bathroom and went back downstairs.

Marcie was already asleep half sitting on the sofa. Gillian covered her with one blanket and wrapped the other around her and curled up as best she could in the wing chair. She hoped she'd hear the little girl if she awoke, but as tired as she was from the night's activities, she might just sleep until Sunday.

"Gillian?" The whispered word woke her.

Opening her eyes, Gillian saw Jenny, already dressed, standing beside the chair, gazing at her, the frown between her eyes clearly showing her worry.

"Hi, sweetie," Gillian said quietly. "What time is it?"

"Almost seven. Why are you and Aunt Marcie here? Daddy's door is shut. Is he sick? He always gets up before me."

Gillian took a minute to come awake before she pushed herself up.

"He's fine," she whispered, glancing at Marcie. "We had an exciting night. My house almost burned down. The fire department was here and I got to watch them fight the fire. Come with me and I'll tell you all about it while I fix breakfast. What would you like?"

She stood and straightened her clothes then followed Jenny into the kitchen.

The sun shone in a cloudless sky. Opening the back door, Gillian heard the low murmur of the surf on the small beach where the sea met the land. She took a deep breath—sea air with a tinge of smoke. She was growing to love this place. Surely she could find a way to stay, if it was the Lord's will.

"I love pancakes. I don't get them during the week because they take so long and we're always in a hurry. But I can have them on Saturdays. Can you fix pancakes?" Jenny asked standing at her elbow.

Marcie entered, yawning. "Hi, punkin'. You just get up?" she asked Jenny.

"Yes. Did you fight the fire at Gillian's house, too?"

"I told her I'd tell her all about it at breakfast," Gillian said. "Want to go over to my place and I'll fix everyone a pancake breakfast? I know where everything is in that kitchen. And any noise we make won't wake Joe."

Marcie checked her watch and made a shrieking noise. "I've got to get to work. I never sleep this late on Saturdays." She gave Jenny a quick kiss on her cheek and looked at Gillian. "You'll be okay?"

"Sure thing. We'll leave Joe a note and head for my house. I have all the ingredients at my place for super-deluxe pancakes."

"Okay. I'll check in with you later." Marcie kissed Jenny and dashed out.

Once the note was written, Jenny and Gillian walked to her house in the early cool air.

Gillian led the little girl toward the back, where they circled the soggy pile of burnt trash. Gillian shivered when she saw the scorched siding on the back of the house. If Joe hadn't discovered the fire in time, her house could have burned to the ground—with her in it!

"Were you scared?" Jenny asked, eying the mound.

"Not at the time, but I think I am now. Your dad saved me—he saved everything. He saw the fire, came to the rescue, and that's how he burned his hands. He caught a burning piece of wood that would have slammed into me. He's a hero. Now his hands are hurt and he'll need extra help over the next few weeks," Gillian said, opening the back door.

Gillian gave Jenny the rundown while she ushered her into the kitchen and shut the door. Thankfully the house didn't smell too strongly of smoke. Later in the day she'd open all the windows and hope the sea breeze would blow fresh air throughout.

Once they had the batter prepared, Gillian began pouring dollops on the griddle.

"Won't Daddy want breakfast, too?" Jenny asked, a frown on her small face as she watched.

"We'll take some over to him."

Not that Gillian had a clue how Joe would eat. Someone would have to feed him.

She almost laughed aloud imagining his expression when he realized that. And since he had saved her from a nasty burn, if not worse, it might be her. He needed help, but she suspected he wouldn't relish any assistance from her.

Gillian enjoyed breakfast with Jenny. They discussed the fire, how the fire trucks had looked. Jenny was angry she hadn't been awake to see them practically in her backyard. She wanted to know all about how they pumped water and stopped the blaze from burning Sophie's house.

Then she changed her interest to Gillian. When she discovered Gillian knew how to dance, she brightened.

"Can you teach me?" Jenny asked. "Then I could be famous and go on TV and everything."

"Not many dancers on TV anymore," Gillian said, serving up a stack of pancakes. She made another batch, sticking them in a warm oven to keep hot. Once they'd finished, she'd take these to Joe. "Besides, what I mostly do is teach aerobics classes."

"What's air-obics class?" Jenny asked.

"Fun times where ladies move to music and get exercise."

"But if there is music, isn't it dancing?"

"Sort of," Gillian said, not sure she could explain the difference to Jenny.

Glancing at the clock, she began to worry again about the meeting with the attorney. Would Joe be awake by then?

Suddenly her phone rang, and she answered it.

"Hello?"

"Gillian? Marcie here. I tried Joe's place first but the phone just rang and rang so I'm thinking he's still asleep. How are things with Jenny?"

"We've finished breakfast. She's a great help." Gillian smiled at the little girl.

"I called Pastor John, and he's going to mobilize the church membership to help Joe out. But in the meantime, are you okay with her being there?"

"Actually, I have an appointment with Julian Greene at ten. If Joe isn't awake by then, I'll bring Jenny with me."

"If you need to, drop her with me off at the café. She can help out. She likes that."

"Sounds more fun than an attorney's office. Will do."

Gillian explained the plan to Jenny once she was off the phone.

"What about Daddy?" the little girl asked.

"We'll check on him and then go to Marcie's. We have to

take him breakfast, after all."

Despite her vow to keep her distance, a hint of anticipation shot through at the thought of seeing Joe again. They hadn't started off very well, but maybe things would change.

Gillian took a quick shower after they'd eaten—making sure to get rid of the smoky smell that clung to her. Dressed in the same black suit she'd worn to the funeral, she hoped it was suitable. It was the most formal, businesslike outfit she'd brought with her, and she wanted to make a good impression on the attorney. After a week in work clothes cleaning the house, it felt good to be wearing something attractive.

Idly, she wondered if Joe would notice. She didn't look like some frumpy cleaning woman.

Taking the plate of hot pancakes from the oven, she called to Jenny. The child had been looking at old photo albums while Gillian dressed.

"You look all dressed up," Jenny said, staring at her.

"I want to look nice to meet with Mr. Greene. Let's go. We'll stop off at your dad's and then head for Marcie's."

Jenny carefully carried the small container of syrup to Gillian's rental car while Gillian handled the plate of pancakes. In no time they were back at the Kincaid home.

Joe was in the kitchen, dressed in a pair of baggy sweatpants and sweatshirt. He needed a shave, the smoke from the fire clung to his skin and hair and he was definitely not in a good mood.

She sighed, suspecting he regretted his good neighborly gesture and wished she'd never come to Rocky Point.

"Wondered when you'd bring her back," he said gruffly.

Gillian smiled, secretly pleased to see he was studying her—he had to see she'd dressed up.

Jenny walked carefully to the table and set the syrup down. "Gillian made you pancakes, Daddy. I had some, and they were d'licious. Do your hands hurt?" She studied the bandages, then stepped closer, as if afraid something might happen to her father again.

He encircled her shoulders and hugged her briefly. "Yeah, they hurt some. But they'll be fine soon."

"Marcie said she'd watch Jenny while I see the attorney," Gillian said, still standing in the doorway, plate in hand.

Joe raised an eyebrow and looked at her. "About the arrival of your father?"

She nodded slowly. "I guess news travels fast in a small town."

"When it concerns one of our own, it does. Sophie was well liked around here. And your father—"

He stopped and glanced at Jenny. "If you're going to go to Marcie's for a while, why don't you take one of your coloring books and crayons?"

"Okay." She ran from the room.

"My father?" Gillian prompted.

"He doesn't exactly have a sterling reputation."

"Oh?" She stepped in and put the plate on the table. "I could reheat them in the microwave," she said.

Joe nudged the covering off the pancakes and stared at them. Gillian saw the moment he realized he couldn't eat them without help. His frustration was clear.

She stepped up to the table, laid down her purse and put the plate in the microwave while she searched for utensils. Finding the silverware, she detoured by the refrigerator and took out the butter. Then she sat beside him, spreading butter on the hot pancakes.

"I can manage," he said.

"No, you can't. Tell me how much butter and syrup you want on them."

He obviously didn't want to comply, but in a moment he grudgingly said, "Lots to both."

Without another word, Gillian prepared them, cut them and scooped a good portion on a fork.

"I got them!" Jenny rushed back into the room, several coloring books clutched in one hand, a huge box of crayons in the other. Jenny came to the table and watched as Gillian scooped up another bite of syrup dripping pancake and held it for Joe to eat. He frowned again, but accepted the food.

"Daddy," she said with a giggle, "You're eating like a baby."

His frown did nothing to stop her giggles. Gillian had trouble keeping from laughing herself.

"I'll do it," he said, reaching for the fork. She moved it out of reach.

"Don't be dumb, Joe. You need to take care of those hands to have them heal as quickly as possible. It's no big deal. Besides, I owe you. If not for me, you wouldn't have gotten burned."

He scowled, but he let her feed him the pancakes.

"Tell me more about my father," she said a minute later,

curious to learn as much about the man as she could.

"What's to tell? He's *your* father."

Chapter Four

"I haven't seen him since I was eight years old," she said, trying to keep the hurt out of her tone.

Not many people's own father wanted nothing to do with them. But Gillian had lived with that knowledge for twenty years. Would meeting him now change anything?

She had long ago stopped wishing for a happy reconciliation. Her mother had died still missing the man she'd given her heart to so many years earlier. How much effort would it have taken for her father to drop them a card at Christmas?

"What?" Joe's surprise was evident.

She shrugged, trying for a nonchalance that would convince him she didn't mind. "He left when I was eight. We never heard from him again. Truth to tell, I thought he must be dead."

"Well, he's not. And up to another scam, unless I miss my guess."

"What's a scam?" Jenny asked, leaning against her father's leg and watching Gillian feed him.

Joe glanced at her. "Nothing you need to worry about. Take your things to Gillian's car. She's about ready to leave."

"You haven't finished eating," she said, peering at his plate.

"I'm getting full. Go on, now."

"Okay. Bye, Daddy." Jenny gave him a kiss and then danced out to the car.

"*Another* scam?" Gillian asked, still feeding him. Who knew when he'd get the chance to eat again. Not before she returned from town, that was for sure.

"He tried to rip off Sophie a few years back. I can't believe Julian didn't take measures then to protect his client. There's no way Sophie would have left him anything."

For the first time since she'd heard of her father's return, Gillian had a glimmer of hope. "So the will he's claiming he has from Sophie might not be a legitimate one?"

"One thing about your old man, he has nerve. My bet is that it's a forgery. I can't believe he'd try something like this after the fiasco ten or twelve years ago. His ego must be bigger than his brain."

"I'll remember that," Gillian said, throwing a quick glance at her watch. "I have to get going. Can I fix you some coffee before I do?"

"No. If you'd call the shop for me and see if Frank is there and ask him to come by, I'd appreciate it."

"Marcie said Pastor John was rallying the troops. I expect you'll have plenty of help before long."

Joe gave a quiet groan as Gillian made the call. When she finished, she hung up and looked at him.

"You don't want help?"

"Looks like I'm going to need it. And get it, whether I

want it or not."

"Remember to be gracious. And grateful," she said, running water over the sticky plate.

"Yes, ma'am," he said.

She flushed and turned to pick up her purse. She had no reason to admonish him. It would be his friends who came to help. She hesitated to leave, but she didn't want to be late.

"See you later," she said as she opened the door.

"Gillian?"

She turned to look over her shoulder at him.

"Thanks."

"I owe you a lot for saving my home."

"I'm just glad we saved it. I appreciate your help with breakfast."

She smiled. "I make a mean sandwich, too," she said.

He slowly smiled, crinkling the skin around his eyes. His unshaven cheeks creased. Gillian caught her breath. "Gotta go," she said and took off before she did something stupid, like cancel her appointment to stay with Joe Kincaid.

Gillian felt more worried than ever when she pushed open the door to the café an hour later. The news from the attorney had not been as reassuring as she had hoped for. The will purportedly written by Sophie naming her grandson as sole heir looked as if it had been properly done. It stated that Sophie left her entire estate to Robert Parker, her grandson.

Julian Greene had told her he would be following up with the attorneys listed on the letterhead to determine if Sophie had indeed gone to Boston two years ago to execute a new will. The big question was why she would have done such a thing, when he had handled her legal affairs since he hung up his shingle.

When asked if she wished to challenge the new will, Gillian hadn't hesitated a second. "You knew Sophie. According to what you told me before, she was very specific in the will and in the letter of instructions she gave you, telling you where I lived and all. I will fight as long as I can to keep the legacy she wanted me to have."

In anticipation of just such a response, Julian had obtained authorization from the probate judge to allow Gillian to continue to occupy the house—pending the investigation.

Her spirits had risen earlier when Joe Kincaid had told her about her father's attempted swindle a number of years ago. Yet with other attorneys involved, this didn't seem like a scam. She wished it were clear cut. But she'd keep the faith until she knew differently.

Scanning the interior of the café when she entered, Gillian noticed it was more crowded than the last time she had been there. Marcie wasn't in sight, nor Jenny.

"May I help you?" One of the pinafore-uniformed waitresses smiled brightly, reaching for a menu.

"I'm looking for Marcie. She has Jenny Kincaid with her. I've come to take Jenny home now."

"Oh, they're in the back. Follow me."

The girl wound her way through the tables heading for the door in the rear.

Halfway through the restaurant, a man rose as Gillian drew near.

"Gillian Parker?" he asked.

She paused, staring at a stranger. He was tall, thin, wearing an expensive suit and silk tie. His dark hair had turned a distinguished gray at the temples. His blue eyes were similar to her own.

"Yes?" Her heart began to pound.

He smiled. Gillian's senses went on alert. The smile was as artificial as the sets on the stages in Vegas. His eyes were assessing, his manner affable. Without another word, she knew who the man was. No wonder he was so good at cons, she thought, when she involuntarily smiled back. Even armed with the knowledge that he was self-centered and untrustworthy, she felt a flash of charisma that charmed.

"I'm Robert Parker—your father."

She noticed the hostess had paused, looking back in puzzlement.

"Why don't you join me?" he said, motioning to one of the vacant chairs at his table. "We have a lot to discuss."

"I don't think we have anything to discuss."

She searched for a connection, a feeling of a family tie. But this man was a stranger to her—merely the man who had broken her mother's heart and left without a word.

The smile lost some of its congeniality. Glancing around at the interested diners, most of whom had given up any pretense of ignoring the scene unfolding before them, he looked back at her.

"For one thing, you're staying in my house. That's something to discuss."

"That is still under debate," she replied.

"What, that you're staying there?"

"That it's *your* house. If you'll excuse me, I meeting someone."

Gillian took steps to follow the hostess when her father's hand gripped her arm, stopping her.

"That's my house now. Pack your things and be out by three today. I'm moving in."

She shrugged her arm free. Stepping closer, she glared into his eyes. "According to my attorney, I have every right to stay right there for the time being."

"We'll see about that," he said, the smile completely gone.

Flushed with anger, Gillian quickly moved to catch up with the hostess.

Grant me patience, Father God. I need it so much. Help me see what I should do, she prayed quickly, hoping to calm her racing heart. .Legally her father might end up with the house. But she wasn't going to give in easily, not after hearing what Joe had to say that morning, nor Mr. Greene's vow to investigate it fully before moving forward.

The fact she was allowed to live there bolstered her hopes.

"How did it go?" Marcie asked when Gillian stepped into the office. Jenny was quietly playing a game on the computer. She looked up and smiled when she saw Gillian.

"Are we ready to go?" she asked, sliding off the chair.

"I am if you are," Gillian said, still rattled from the confrontation in the restaurant. She had longed to meet her father for years. Had hoped there'd be an instant connection. Instead, she felt only anger and disappointment. Maybe the Lord had been merciful in having him absent from her life.

"I'm ready," Jenny said, her books and crayons gathered in hand. "Thanks for watching me, Aunt Marcie, but I have to go home. My dad needs me to take care of him. He can't even eat by himself. Gillian had to feed him."

"Well, then he will need you there to help him. Tell him I'll bring dinner later, okay? Plan to join us, Gillian, I'll bring plenty."

"You don't have to do that. I can cook for the Kincaids. Besides, I can make some great Tex-Mex meals."

"Something different, for sure," Marcie said.

As Gillian drove back toward home, Jenny said "Aunt Marcie's nice, isn't she?"

"She is. And it's a good thing your dad has her and others from your church. He's going to need a lot of support over the next few weeks."

"Aren't you going to help?" Jenny asked.

"Yes, as long as he needs me. But it's not the same thing as family."

"Oh, then we need to get Uncle Zack."

"Uncle Zack?"

"Uh-huh, he's Daddy's brother. He's family, isn't he?"

"Yes, he's family. Where does Uncle Zack live?"

"I don't know. Daddy e-mails him, but he hardly never comes home."

"Hardly ever," Gillian corrected absently. "He'd want to know about your dad's injury. Then I bet he comes home to help."

"That would be super. Can we write and tell him?" Jenny asked, bouncing as much as the seat belt would allow.

Gillian shrugged. "Your dad could, I guess."

"No, I want to surprise him," Jenny said.

"Do you know his e-mail address?" Gillian asked.

"Yes, I send him letters, too, but mostly Daddy has to help me cause I can't type so good."

"Since your dad won't be typing anytime soon, you and I can let your uncle know," Gillian promised.

Joe Kincaid was sitting on a recliner, watching TV, when Gillian and Jenny walked in. A man Gillian had never met before was sprawled on the sofa. Jenny ran to greet her father, being careful of his hands.

"Are you better yet?" she asked.

Joe hugged his child and smiled. "Not yet. But I'm getting there. How was your morning at Marcie's?" He glanced up at Gillian. "Thanks for bringing her home. This is Frank Halson. He works for me at the shop."

"Howdy, ma'am," Frank said, standing.

Gillian smiled and came forward to shake his hand. "Hello, Frank. It's nice to meet you."

"Gillian lives in Sophie's house now. She's been cleaning and cleaning," Jenny said, from her perch on her daddy's lap. "It doesn't have any curtains."

"Well, I'm sure Gillian will fix that up soon," Frank said.

He nodded at Joe. "If you don't need anything more, I'll head out. I want to run by the shop before going home."

"Appreciate your help, Frank."

The man looked embarrassed. "No problem. See you, Jenny. Nice to meet you, Gillian," he said as he left.

"I'm going home to change. Then I'll fix us some lunch."

"You don't have to cook for us," Joe said.

"Maybe not. But I want to. Do you like grilled-cheese sandwiches?" She was happy when around him. It was a joy to cook for more than herself and see how appreciative he was. She hoped he liked her food, it wasn't much. More to stay around him than extraordinary nutrition.

He nodded. "I like your company more."

Gillian smiled at that. Those words encouraged her more than anything.

"How do your hands feel?" she asked.

"The left better than the right." He held up his hand and flexed his fingers slightly. "Hardly notice the pain," he said.

"Good try. I know burns can really hurt. Want me to take Jenny with me until lunch?"

"No. She'll be fine here."

"I'll be back."

"Plan to stay awhile," he said.

Joe watched her leave. He had mixed emotions about his new neighbor. The more he knew her, the more confused he became. She looked like high maintenance, yet she acted down to earth. He had yet to hear any complaints from her about Rocky Point or the disrepair of Sophie's house. In the past, he'd insisted on helping Sophie with some things like wiring and plumbing, over her protests. But he knew better than most how determined Sophie'd been to make it on her own as long as she could. He'd seen how hard it had become for her to keep up the house. Gillian had a huge task ahead of her.

Now she offered lunch. It was the first time anyone had cooked for him since Pamela died. He smiled and tried to ignore the jump his stomach made at the thought of seeing her again. He was used to fending for himself. It was a novel experience to have a neighbor do for him. A *beautiful* neighbor, at that.

He glanced at his daughter. "So, tell me what you did at the café," he said, hoping to hear a little more about Gillian Parker.

Gillian drove home and went inside to change. Once in comfortable jeans and a warm sweater, she went out back to survey the damage to her trash pile.

If she'd had any suspicions it would burn, she would have called for the trash to be picked up each day. Or at least would have stacked it on the edge of the bluff instead of behind the house. The pile was soggy and smelled of smoke. Here and there a recognizable piece of fabric or wooden leg stuck out, but the majority of the pile was gray and black, charred and burned and soaked.

Before Gillian headed back for the Kincaid house, she called a handyman who removed trash. He knew instantly who she was and where to come for the pickup and promised to do so first thing Monday morning.

Back at the Kincaid house, Gillian found lunch to be unexpectedly fun. She kept watching the interaction between Joe and his daughter, a touch of envy sweeping through her at their closeness. This morning had proved the vast chasm between Gillian and her own father.

As if conscious of her expression, Joe looked at her and held her gaze. Her heart began to pound. She smiled, trying to appear at ease.

"Need anything else?" she asked to cover her feeling of confusion.

She'd prepared tomato soup and the sandwiches. Alternating between eating her own meal and feeding Joe, she'd felt closer to the man than before. He took her ministrations with good grace.

He glanced at the empty soup bowl and empty plate. "Nothing more except perhaps some more water."

She jumped up to refill their glasses. Jenny finished her meal. "Can I go to Melissa's?" she asked. "Her mom will come get me. I told her you hurted your hands and can't drive me."

Joe nodded. "I'll call her mom and verify."

Gillian returned with the water. She had stuck a straw into Joe's so he could drink without help.

He looked at her. "Would you mind calling Shirley for me? The number is in the notebook next to the phone. Just make sure it's okay for Jenny to come over."

Gillian placed the call. She told Shirley who she was and why she was calling

"I've been meaning to stop by to meet you, but you know how hectic things can get," Shirley said. "Welcome to Rocky Point. I'm sorry about your grandmother. Sophie was a member of our Tuesday morning Bible study group for years. We really miss her."

Gillian still wasn't sure how to respond when faced with friends of her great-grandmother. "Thanks. I'll walk Jenny out when you get here and say hello."

"Great. I'll be there in less than ten minutes. Melissa's happy they'll spend the afternoon together. I'll bring some cinnamon rolls for tomorrow. I know Joe won't be cooking for a while."

Gillian had time to clean the kitchen before Shirley arrived to pick up Jenny. Joe sat at the table and watched her as she put the food away and wiped the table and counter, talking about Jenny's friendship with Melissa.

She glanced over at him from time to time. It felt right to be sharing routine tasks like lunch and cleaning up afterwards.

When Shirley arrived, with Melissa, Jenny raced out the door. Gillian followed to meet Shirley. They chatted for a few minutes about Joe and his injuries. Shirley invited Gillian to attend Trinity Church in the morning. Gillian told her she planned to do so and would look for her there.

Once Jenny left, Gillian went back inside.

"I'm off," she said.

Joe rose and walked to her. "Thank you again for lunch."

"I was happy to do it. Do you like chili? I make great spicy chili. I thought we could have that for dinner."

"Sounds great. What are your plans this afternoon?"

"I want to go through Sophie's office. I'm so confused about whether she wanted me to have the house or if that other will leaving it to my dad shows a change of heart. Maybe I'll find something in her desk. I've put off going through that to get the rest of the house in some kind of order. I didn't think it would be top priority."

"Want some company?"

She nodded, suddenly pleased he wasn't pushing her away. "I'd love it."

Not counting the attorney and Marcie, Joe was the closest

thing she had to a friend in Rocky Point. She'd met a dozen or more people in town, but so far there hadn't been enough time to forge friendships.

Gillian and Joe walked to her house and went straight to the small room where Sophie had kept her records.

"You've done a lot with the house," Joe said as they walked through the sparkling rooms.

"No curtains, as Jenny said. But every window has a wonderful view. I don't want to cover them up."

"It's your place. Decorate it as you like."

"I hope it's going to be mine. I've never owned a home. I've always rented apartments."

She looked around with affection for the gift that might be hers. The small room that served as an office had a desk and three chairs.

"Tell me about Sophie," she said. "I want to know everything."

Joe sat in one of the chairs and began with memories he had of Sophie when he'd been a young boy.

Gillian worked as he talked and quickly found files neatly labeled going back thirty years or more. She brought in a large trash can and began to review what each file held. Some were recipes that looked interesting. Some files had old electrical bills dating years earlier. Those Gillian tossed. Any files that looked like the attorney should check out, she put in one pile.

What surprised her most was when she withdrew the thick file labeled "Gillian."

"Joe," she said. "Look at this. It seems Sophie knew all about me."

Gillian held up a sheaf of papers. "A detective agency wrote an annual report on me."

She ruffled through the pages. "He even has my grades from school. How did he managed that?"

Gillian leaned back against the chair, almost in tears.

Sophie Parker had known about her all her life and yet had never tried once to contact her. Not even when her mother died and she'd been alone in the world. Why not?

"So she did know you. I think it strengthens the case that she wanted you to have this home," Joe said, reading some of the pages.

"But why not contact me? I'd have given anything to know I had a great-grandmother living."

"Look in the back of the file. Maybe there's a letter or something," he offered.

She shook her head after looking. "Nothing." She looked at him. "She never said anything to you about me?"

"No, but we weren't friends that way. She was more like a grandmother to me and Jenny. Maybe some of her friends know more. You'll meet them tomorrow at church. I'm sure if she told anyone, it would be either Maud Stevens or Caroline Everett. Sophie and Maud went to school together and were friends all their lives."

"Were either of them at the funeral?" she asked.

"Caroline was. I didn't see Maud. But she's elderly herself. Maybe it was too much for her."

"Guess I'll see if I can meet them and ask," she said.

"Come on. Let's take a walk," he said, standing.

She looked up. "Where?"

"Along the bluff. I think you've done enough exploration for today. The fresh air will feel good."

She put the folder on the desk and stood.

"You're right. I can't change the past, only try to understand it, I guess. I'm up for something more lively right now. And while we walk, maybe you can tell me what fire guns are."

"Is that science fiction?" he asked as they left the house by the back door.

"Jenny said you have fire guns at the shop."

He laughed. "Probably means the acetylene torches for welding."

They headed for the bluff and turned toward Rocky Point.

"Come by the shop sometime and I'll show you my fire guns."

Gillian glanced at him and smiled.

Joe looked around. The day seemed brighter than before. The grass was greener, the sky bluer. It had been years since he'd walked with a woman just to enjoy the day and each other's company. Since he and Pamela were in high school.

And look where that had led.

"That was fast," she said, breaking him out of his thoughts.

"What?"

"Your mood change. For a second you looked on top of the world, then like you'd lost your last best friend."

He deliberately shook off the thoughts about his failed marriage. He'd enjoy today with Gillian and worry about the future later.

"It's nothing. Tell me about Las Vegas."

"Changing the subject?"

"And finding out more about my new neighbor in the process," he said with a grin.

He was growing fascinated by a beautiful woman. As long as he kept things casual, they'd be fine. He knew better than to plan on happily ever after. That was more for fairy tales than real life.

The afternoon was beautiful. A slight breeze blew in from the sea. The water sparkled beneath the sunshine. Joe felt young and carefree for the first time in a long while. He was walking with a beautiful woman, getting to know her, sharing some of his life with her. It would be enough for today.

He walked Gillian back to her house while she gathered the ingredients for dinner, then they walked to his place. Jenny would be home for dinner so it was easier to make it in his kitchen. His hands didn't hurt as much. The pain medication was working. So he was able to enjoy being with Gillian as she bustled around preparing the chili. He liked watching her work. She concentrated on each task, then looked up and flashed that bright smile. Next item to take care of, then that smile. He could count on it each time and each time he wanted to see it last forever.

Gillian found preparing dinner with someone standing around and talking with her more fun than she expected. She was careful when preparing the meal not to get distracted and forget to add an ingredient, or add something twice. But it was hard to keep from looking at Joe. He seemed more relaxed, though his hands had to hurt. The walk had been delightful.

And seemed to bring them closer. Or was that her wishful thinking?

She missed her friends from Nevada. Maybe Joe would fill one of the empty spots. Maybe in time become more than a friend. She'd love to fall in love and have a large family to love and grow with.

Did he want more children?

She began making the corn bread, firmly changing the thoughts on her mind. They were just becoming friends—too early to plan a anything together.

Their walk had buoyed her spirits. Joe had a way with a story that had her laughing at the outrageous tales he told. Her interest in his shop had increased as she learned more about his love of restoring vintage cars. He touched on little of a personal nature, but she hadn't noticed, enchanted with the man and his way with words.

Jenny arrived home just as the corn bread was coming out of the oven.

Dinner turned out to be fun.

Gillian had Jenny help with the salad. Joe volunteered to taste test the chili for her and she let him, holding the spoon out to him, her gaze locked with his. Her cheeks felt flushed.

Laughter rang out often. By the time they sat down to the table for dinner, Gillian felt as at ease in his kitchen as she did in her own.

"Do you want to say the blessing?" Joe asked.

"Your home, your blessing," she replied.

"Father, we thank You for today. For the beautiful world You made for us. We thank You for bringing Gillian into our lives to enrich and

expand it. For the trials and hardships we face, we ask You to be with us. Thank You for this food and for all who prepared it. May it nourish our bodies as our fellowship renews our spirits. Through Jesus we pray, Amen."

Gillian smiled at Joe, her heart expanding with emotion. She liked a man who could pray so sincerely aloud. Some members of her church were too shy to.

"Tell daddy about the horse," Jenny said, looking at Gillian.

"What horse?"

"You know, the horse you're going to get because you always wanted one and I can ride it!"

Joe frowned and spoke before Gillian could reply. "You're not riding any horse."

Gillian and Jenny looked at him.

"In the first place, I'm not getting a horse. And second, I'd never let her ride without your permission," Gillian said.

Joe stared back at her. "It's dangerous."

Jenny kicked her chair. "It's fun. Melissa and I went to see her pony. We couldn't ride it, but if she asks me again, I want to."

"I'll need to make it clear to Shirley," he muttered.

"They'd take precautions," Gillian said gently. "All girls want to have a horse. I sure did."

"Wanting, dreaming, that's one thing. Actually getting on one is something else. Maybe when you're older," he said.

"You always say that."

"Better than no," Gillian said, hoping to smooth things over.

"The chili burns my mouth," Jenny complained.

"I tried to tone it down. Is it too hot?" Gillian asked, stricken.

"Pretty spicy, but probably because we aren't used to it," Joe said.

"Hey, you taste-tested it all afternoon. You can't complain."

Jenny laughed. "I like it, but I need corn bread."

When they'd finished eating, Jenny ran up to her room. Gillian did the dishes while Joe leaned against the counter watching her. For a few moments she could imagine being married and having a family. Her husband could spend time with her at the end of the day and they'd go over what they'd done since they'd last seen each other.

"Gillian, can you come see my room?" Jenny called from the top of the stairs a little later.

"Go ahead," he said. "She wants you to see it. I'll be in the living room catching up on the news."

"We need to write to Uncle Zack," Jenny whispered when Gillian stepped into her room. It was decorated in pink and blue. The coverlet on the bed was frilly and pretty. The furnishings were sturdy and practical, painted a bright white to contrast with the light-blue walls. Her view was out the back toward the sea.

Against one wall her child's desk held a laptop computer. "I got the computer from Daddy's room. But I have to take it back before he knows what we're doing. I want it to be a surprise."

Gillian sat at the desk and saw that Jenny knew enough to

log on. It was her typing skills that were still lacking. She was only seven.

"What should I say?" Gillian asked when she had the mail program open.

"Tell uncle Zack daddy needs him. He has to come home," Jenny said.

Gillian promptly typed a message she hoped would bring Joe's brother home.

Why hadn't he contacted Zack himself? Was there more to the family dynamics than she knew? Joe hadn't mentioned having a brother. Yet Jenny was sure Zack would come straight home once he knew Joe needed him.

Chapter Five

The phone rang early Sunday morning. Gillian had finished dressing for church. She ran downstairs to answer. She'd have to get an upstairs extension or give people her cell number.

"Hello?" she said.

"Hi, Gillian. Can you give me a ride to church? Daddy said he'd call Marcie, but I want to go with you." Jenny's voice came through clearly.

"Sure thing. Let me talk to your daddy."

A moment later she heard the deep voice. "This is Joe."

Short and to the point.

"I'm happy to give Jenny a ride to church. Does she normally go to Sunday School?"

"Yes, we do attend Bible study prior to the main service."

"Great, what time should I pick her up?"

"In about fifteen minutes."

"I'm all ready to go, so I'll swing by now. Can I get you anything when I'm in town?"

"No. I'll tell Jenny." He hung up without another word.

Not that there was anything special she wanted to hear. She'd had fun yesterday with Joe, and she hoped he felt the same.

Jenny chatted away as she rode with Gillian to church. "And my friend Becky has a new bike. I'm the only one in the class who doesn't have one."

"That's tough," Gillian said.

Was money a concern in the Kincaid household? She wouldn't have thought it from the way their house was furnished and the nice clothing Jenny wore.

Still, one never knew. Many of the children she'd taught in Sunday School had bicycles and they were younger than Jenny. Maybe money was an issue.

"Maybe you could get a good secondhand bike at the thrift store," she suggested.

"Daddy said I can't have a bike."

Her tone was so morose Gillian had to hide a smile. She felt for Jenny. She remembered being a bit different from other children when growing up.

"So ask your dad if you can help out around my house and I'll pay you. Then you can save up for it yourself," she suggested.

"You mean it?" Jenny asked with excitement, sitting up. Her entire demeanor changed.

"Sure, as long as it's all right with your father."

Gillian hoped Joe would agree. She'd welcome the company when scrubbing down walls, if nothing else.

When they arrived at Trinity Church, the parking lot was almost full. Gillian found a space and held Jenny's hand as they walked into the old church. In seconds Jenny spotted some friends and pulled away, calling over her shoulder that she'd meet Gillian later.

"Oh, you must be Sophie's granddaughter," an older woman said as Jenny left.

"I'm Gillian Parker," she acknowledged. "Actually her great-granddaughter."

"I'm Caroline Everett. Sophie was a dear friend. I miss her so much."

Gillian smiled, wishing again she'd had the chance to meet her great-grandmother.

"How nice that you've come. Our Sunday School is starting soon. You won't want to be in my class—we're all too old. There's a nice young adult class that would be perfect. Come on, I'll take you there. And for church service, do join me. Sophie and I sat next to each other for years. I don't expect you to sit with me every time, of course, but at least let me introduce you around this morning. Oh, Maud will be so sorry to miss you. She broke her hip, you know. She's in a rehab center in Portland, but she plans to get back home soon."

"That's very kind of you," Gillian said, following the woman into the Sunday School rooms. As they walked to the classes, Caroline introduced her to almost everyone they passed. Finally reaching the fourth door, Caroline led her in and introduced her to the teacher.

"Mind, now, I expect to sit with you at church," Mrs. Everett said before she left for her class.

Gillian enjoyed meeting all the twenty-somethings in the Bible study. They were friendly and welcoming. Two suggested they get together for coffee some morning and get better acquainted.

The morning service was a delight—from the familiar hymns to the message Pastor John gave. Afterward, Gillian lingered in the large lobby chatting with some of the people she'd met while waiting for Jenny.

Shirley had come up to reissue her invitation to the Tuesday morning Bible study for women. Caroline had introduced her to several other friends of Sophie's. And Melissa waved to her from across the lobby.

Marcie came over and gave her a hug. "Come by the café after church some time. We always have a Sunday special," she said.

When Jenny ran over to her, she was waving a picture colored with crayons.

"This is for you!" she said, holding it for Gillian. "Hello, Mrs. Everett," she said politely.

"Hello, Jenny. You look lovely today."

"I dressed myself. My daddy hurted his hands."

"I heard. You'll be a big help to him until he's better."

Jenny nodded and looked at Gillian. "Can we go now?"

Gillian's head was spinning with all the introductions. She'd never keep everything straight. But the warmth of the welcomes had been heartfelt. More than ever, she now felt she'd made the right decision to come to Rocky Point.

Turning into Joe's driveway a short time later felt familiar and comfortable, and she couldn't deny the rising anticipation at seeing Joe again.

Entering the kitchen with Jenny a few minutes later, she was disappointed not to have him greet them.

"Should I fix lunch?" Gillian asked.

"Yes, please. I need to change out of my Sunday clothes first in case I spill something on them," Jenny said.

A moment later Gillian heard her running through the house yelling for her father.

She had pulled out sliced turkey, cheese and bread to prepare sandwiches when Joe came into the kitchen.

"You don't have to do that," he said.

She turned and smiled, struck again by his masculine looks. He needed to shave, but the beginning of a beard looked very appealing. He wore baggy sweats, but she could still see his broad shoulders and fit body.

"I'm happy to do it," she said, turning back to the food. "One or two sandwiches? There's a bit of chili left, if you want that, too."

"Two. And I'd love some more chili. So, how was church?"

Gillian told him about all the people she'd met, her favorable reaction to the Bible study class and updated him on Maud Stevens' whereabouts.

"I hadn't heard about Maud. But she'll be okay, right?"

"Mrs. Everett thinks so. Everyone was so friendly."

"What did you expect?"

"More closed ranks, because it's a small town."

"Depends on the person. You're considered one of our own, being Sophie's great-granddaughter."

She nodded.

He leaned against the doorjamb crossing his arms across his chest, careful not to press against his hands.

"Several people from church sent their regards through me," Gillian said, looking as though she were trying to recall all the names.

Joe wondered what Mrs. Everett and the others at church had thought about the gorgeous woman from Las Vegas. He studied Gillian as she prepared a meal for him and Jenny. She looked so out of place in his rather plain kitchen. Yet she was humming softly as she placed the turkey on the bread and checked the chili heating in the microwave. He recognized the hymn.

"How are your hands today?" she asked a moment later.

"Not too bad. I'll go back to the doc's tomorrow for a bandage change and to have him check them again."

"I can give you a ride," she offered.

"Thanks. Appreciate it."

Gillian tilted her head and looked at him. Maybe she should push her luck just a bit while he seemed so agreeable.

"May I hire Jenny for a few hours a week to help me around the house?"

"Help you do what? She's seven. Too young to work."

"I merely want to help her earn some money. I think children should know not everything in life comes free. And to give her a chance to earn a bit."

"What does she need money for? I provide everything she needs."

"Not a bike. Or pony, come to think of it," Gillian said. Placing the first sandwich on a plate, she cut it in half.

"She doesn't need either one," he snapped. Maybe he should have a talk with his daughter about keeping family business private.

"Well, maybe *needs* is a bit strong, but if she is the only girl in her class not to have a bike, that can set her apart. I know money can be tight. So I thought—"

"You thought I couldn't afford a bike, so you'd step in and make sure she had one? And teach her that money can buy anything, and always go after the big bucks?"

Gillian turned and stared at him. "What are you talking about? I wanted to help. If you can't afford to buy—"

"Get your facts straight before you butt in next time," he said, pushing away from the door and walking closer to her. She stepped back one step, watching him in surprise.

"Such as?"

"I can afford to buy my daughter anything she needs. What she does *not* need is a bike. Do you know how many children are injured riding bikes each year? Or how many die in traffic fatalities because some driver didn't see them?"

Gillian was taken aback. Was he that scared for Jenny's safety?

"How many? How many have been killed in Rocky Point? Maybe the traffic is worse in summer, but today I passed three cars on the ride from the church to home. You're telling me you're worried about her getting hit by a car in this small town? That's unlikely."

"But not impossible."

"Children have been riding bicycles for generations. Don't you realize that you single her out as different by not letting her have one when all the other children do?"

"I don't care about the other children, and I don't want to

talk about it. I've made up my mind."

"Joe, I can't believe you won't let her ride with her friends."

"Maybe when she's older."

"The other children don't have to wait," she pointed out.

"I can't risk her life. I almost lost her once."

Gillian took a breath. What was he talking about? "How?"

"My wife took her in a car when Jenny was two, there was a bad car accident. My wife, Pamela, died. Jenny was injured. It was touch and go. I almost lost her. I can't risk her life on frivolous bicycles or horses or any of the dangerous things she wants to try."

"Have you explained that to her?"

He shook his head.

Gillian reached out and rubbed his arm lightly. "Tell her. Offer her safe things to do that will allow her to be equal with her classmates. She needs that. I know. I was always odd girl out in school because I didn't have a dad when all my friends did. It's hard, Joe, to be different."

She didn't really have the right to tell him how to handle his life. But she ached for Jenny's disappointment.

"I'll think about it," he said a moment later.

When her hand dropped, he stepped closer and surprised her by wrapping his arms around her. "It's not easy being a single dad," he said.

She relished the warm hug, which was over too soon. Smiling brightly she nodded. "I'm sure it's not. But you're doing great. She's a delightful child."

Once lunch was over, Gillian returned home. She changed her clothes and then put on the radio and set to cleaning another room. Work would banish the fluttery feelings she had around Joe and give her something to do.

Gillian was glad for the break when the doorbell rang an hour later. She'd been working nonstop, and her back was beginning to feel strained. Glancing around the spare bedroom before heading downstairs, she smiled in satisfaction. It was looking much better. She could just picture frilly white Priscilla curtains and a light-blue paint on the walls.

When she opened the door, Gillian was surprised to see her father standing on the wooden porch.

They stared at each for a moment, then her father smiled and said, "Are you going to invite me in?"

"Should I?" According to what the attorney had said, she had the right of occupancy. Should she let Robert Palmer in the house?

"Or we can sit out here, if you'd prefer," he said easily, as if guessing her doubts.

She was instantly suspicious. His demeanor was a complete about-face from at the café. The charm factor was back.

"I can bring out something to drink, if you like," she said, still holding the door partway closed, mixed emotions churning. For years she'd longed for the close relationship Joe had with his daughter, yet she didn't trust this man.

"Not necessary."

He turned and went to sit in one of the Adirondack chairs

flanking a small wooden table. With the house sheltering them from the ocean breeze, it was pleasant, not too cold. The sun peeked beneath the overhang. So far the chairs remained in shade.

Gillian closed the door behind her and sat in the second chair. She studied the man who had deserted her and her mother so many years ago.

"My mother is dead," she said.

He looked pained. "I know that. I learned about it not long after her death. She never remarried."

"She loved you."

He looked away. "She was a beautiful woman. We had a lot of fun together." He looked back at her. "You have her coloring and height. Perhaps you're even prettier."

"Why did you leave?"

"I wanted to make it big. Having a family held me back."

Gillian winced at his comment. *She*'d held him back. He'd been content in his marriage to her mother before she came along. Eight years with a child had been too much.

The silence stretched on for a couple of moments. Finally she asked, "And *did* you make it big?"

He shrugged. "I've had some setbacks. But now I have a chance to change all that. Sophie was my grandmother. She and I were close when I was a boy. Then my mother moved us west. But the blood tie was always there."

"She's related to me as well," Gillian said, knowing where this was leading.

"She never met you. I stayed with her summers when I was growing up."

"And your point is?"

"The house is mine. She wrote another will—by an independent lawyer, not one who was influencing her. I'll prevail on the inheritance. If you leave now, I'll cut you in on the sale price."

"You're planning to sell the house?" she asked, astonished. She'd heard that rumor, but it was so precious to her she hadn't really believed he planned to sell their family's home.

"I'm not living here in Rocky Point," he said. He glanced up at the front of the house. "The place is in bad shape, but I'm sure someone would buy it for the land. The view's amazing. She owned over two acres, enough space to build a small condominium complex for vacationers."

"That would change everything. Besides, I don't see Rocky Point as precisely a hot spot of tourist activity." Which was one of the reasons she liked it. "This is our family home."

"Which would eat up a ton of money trying to keep it up." He glanced disparagingly around. "It's falling apart."

"No, it's not. It's actually sound. Just needs some cosmetic work."

She already loved the old house, its character and its charm.

"Which given the size of the place would still cost a lot. Best to sell it as is and hope the land brings in the money."

"I'm not selling." She raised her chin a notch. She'd fight for her home.

"Not your decision," he said easily.

A movement caught her eye and she looked beyond her

father to see Joe walking toward them.

Robert looked over his shoulder and frowned. "Is that Joe Kincaid? What happened to his hands?"

"There was fire in the back and he got burned trying to help me," she replied.

She felt a wave of gratitude that he was coming. "You know him?" she asked. Had he suspected she needed support?

Robert shrugged. "Know him a bit, from when I stayed with Sophie a few years back. He was always poking his nose in where it wasn't wanted."

No doubt protecting his neighbor, Gillian thought.

Joe reached the porch and stepped up. "Robert. I heard you were in town."

"Joe. You still have that fix-it car shop?"

"I do car restorations."

If he was annoyed at the put-down, he didn't show it. Gillian hoped she was as good at not showing how she felt about her father. It had been a disconcerting meeting so far. She wanted to go inside, lock the door and have some chocolate.

Joe leaned casually against one of the posts, studying Robert. "I heard you're claiming Sophie wrote a will in Boston leaving the place to you."

"That's a fact."

"Odd, don't you think?"

"That a grandson would inherit? I don't think that's odd."

Robert stood up, as if he resented the younger man standing over him.

"What's odd is Sophie using an attorney instead of Julian,

who handled all her affairs both before and after that alleged trip to Boston. She never mentioned a new will to him. Even left a letter of instruction on how to locate Gillian."

"Alleged! I have documents to prove it!"

Joe shrugged. "Not my business. Just curious."

"No one cares what you think, Kincaid. This is my inheritance and I'm claiming it."

"So we'll be neighbors," Joe said.

"He plans to sell to a developer if he gets the house," Gillian said.

Joe smiled. "Not likely. This is zoned for single-family dwellings. And there isn't a person on the Board of Supervisors who would vote to change it."

Robert drew himself up. He was still shorter than Joe. And at least twenty years older. Even with a scruffy beard and dressed in sweats, compared to Robert's elegant suit, Joe came off the better man in Gillian's eyes.

She felt the warmth within grow that Joe was championing her side.

"This is getting me nowhere. We'll see what the future holds," Robert said. He gave a curt nod to Gillian, brushed past Joe and went out to his car. Joe turned and watched as he drove away.

Turning back, he dropped into the chair Robert had recently occupied.

"Trying to intimidate you?" he asked.

"Maybe. But it didn't work. Julian said I have a better than even chance, even if she did change her will. Which he doesn't believe she did."

"Too easy to check. Maybe Robert did get her to give him the old family home. Especially since she never met you," Joe said pensively.

"She has the detective's reports over the years. I think she meant for me to have it. At least I pray that was her intent. It means so much to me."

"Something to sell and have the money to fall back on?" he murmured.

"Don't confuse me with my father. I'm settling in here. That's the difference between him and me—I'm here, the good Lord willing, for the rest of my life."

Joe leaned back and looked at her. Her hair was a reddish-gold cloud about her face and shoulders. In contrast, the clothes she wore looked as if they belonged in a rag heap. There was a streak of dirt down one cheek. Interest stirred. He wanted to know all about Gillian Parker. And wondered if he could trust that she was here for good.

Glancing away before he forgot what he'd come to say, he took a breath and began.

"I shouldn't have blown up at you about Jenny and the bike. I just imagine the worst whenever I'm away from her. She's so precious. And kids get to playing and not paying attention. Who knows what could happen?"

"I understand. I hope you see I'm looking out for her, as well. People can be injured and hurt in other ways beside physically. Were you ever the odd man out? What am I saying? Of course not."

He tried to understand her viewpoint, but then the picture of his baby girl scraped up and unconscious five years ago came to mind.

"Life can be scary."

"The Lord takes care of His own," she said softly.

He nodded. He knew that. Could he trust in the Lord to watch over his baby?

"So maybe in a year or two we'll see about a bike," he said. It still sounded dangerous to him.

"And get a pony?" Gillian asked, her eyes twinkling.

"Man, she's still harping on that pony? Since her friend Melissa got one, that's been the topic of dinner discussions more times than I can count. I told Shirley I don't want Jenny riding it. She said she won't let other children ride until after Melissa has bonded with the pony."

Gillian smiled, and Joe watched the transformation on her face. She was beyond beautiful when she smiled. Her eyes lit up and her entire face seemed to radiate happiness. He liked it. He liked her smiling at him.

He broke off staring at her and looked out over the front yard, idly noting the grass was beginning to look unkempt, the flower beds scraggly. Sophie wouldn't have liked that. She used to hire Marvin Henny to keep the lawn neat. Had dealt with the flowers on her own. Did Gillian know about Henny? Or anything about gardening?

"Does she remember her mother?" Gillian asked.

Joe looked back in surprise. "What?"

"If she was just two, my guess is she doesn't remember her," Gillian said softly. "I wonder if that's a good thing or not. I remember my dad, playing with me, laughing. Then one day he was gone. Would it have been better if I didn't have any memories?"

"Pamela was on her way to New York. She wanted more from life than what I could provide here in Rocky Point. I never told Jenny she was leaving me. So far I've been able to tell her only good things about my wife." The words were wrung from him.

Gillian looked surprised.

For a moment he felt a flash of gratitude that she didn't immediately say she knew why his wife had left. But then, she hardly knew him.

"I'm doubly sorry, then. For your loss and Jenny's."

He shrugged. "It was a long time ago."

"Some pain never goes away."

He rose. "Well, I'll be heading back. Just came over when I saw Robert pull up."

"Thank you for being here," she said, standing as well.

Gillian watched him cross the land between the two houses. She didn't agree with his decision regarding Jenny's learning new things, but she had never been a parent. Obviously he had to do what he felt right for his own daughter.

Would she ever have a daughter? Or a son? She'd like to find someone to share her life with, to have babies with and raise them with love and laughter in this old home. Lately, that nebulous someone was slowly taking on the features of Joe. He'd been kind and helpful—even putting himself in danger for her safety. But she thought there was more to him. Would he ever find enough about her to love?

Slowly she returned to her tasks, praying again that the

Lord's plan was for her to inherit the old house and not her father. Since he only wanted to sell, maybe she could work some kind of deal to buy it from him if he was awarded the place.

Which meant she needed to get a job soon. Her savings wouldn't cover the cost, and without any source of income, she doubted any bank would lend her money.

Rocky Point didn't have a gym. She'd ask Marcie next time she saw her if she knew of any exercise studios in neighboring towns that might need an instructor. She'd pray today about her future and hope to learn what her heavenly Father wished for her.

Chapter Six

Gillian brought the morning paper and her cup of hot tea to the front porch. It was still cool and she wore jeans and a sweatshirt. Hard to believe it would be in the high nineties in Vegas today. She was glad to escape the heat.

She'd check out any available jobs in the local paper and then finish working on the bedroom she'd begun yesterday. She was impatient to buy new bedding, paint and some new curtains but was conscious of the uncertainty about the future of the house.

Turning immediately to the help wanted section, she looked quickly through the scant listings. Nothing suitable. Sighing softly, she leaned back and sipped the hot tea.

Show me the path You've designed for me, I pray, Lord. Do I get this house? Should I use it for Your glory, or have You something else in store for me? I pray for guidance. Let me know Your will, Father.

Peace descended, and she was content to relax and enjoy the beauty of the Maine spring.

Would her mother have liked this area of the country? She'd been from Southern California, had gone to Vegas when Gillian's father had moved them there—seeking the big deal.

What was wrong with steady, hard work to enjoy life's

blessings? Gillian wondered. Those who constantly tried for instant wealth usually failed.

Would her life have been drastically different had her father stayed? Or would it have been worse, moving from place to place, always seeking the gold ring. *Lay not your treasures upon earth*, the Bible said. Her father needed better grounding in the Scriptures, she thought.

An old pickup truck turned into her driveway. Gillian didn't recognize the driver. The man who stepped out a moment later looked to be in his late fifties. Dressed in faded, baggy jeans and a dark flannel shirt, the odd hat with dozens of fishing lures caught her attention.

"Gillian Parker?" he asked as he approached the porch, looking at the flower beds in passing.

"That's right." She stood and went to meet him on the shallow steps.

"Marvin Henny. I took care of the yard for Mrs. Parker. Not the roses, mind. That was her domain. She won some fancy prizes at the county fair with her roses."

Gillian looked at the scraggly bushes and few weeds starting in the flower beds. She wasn't sure which were weeds and which were flowers. "I've never had a garden before. I've always lived in apartments. I have no idea what to do."

He rubbed his chin a moment and then nodded. "I could take that on as well. Might not get the prizes your grandmother won, but the gardens will look good, that I guarantee."

"I'd appreciate it. So, the entire yard, lawn, flower beds and all?"

He nodded, glancing at the grass that was long overdue for a trim. "I'll come on Thursdays if that suits you. It was my day for Mrs. Parker."

"How much?" Gillian asked. She never thought about the yard before. She'd been too focused on the interior.

He gave her a sum she thought amazingly low and she quickly agreed. Another step on the path to home ownership, she smiled to herself.

He nodded and turned back toward his truck. The phone rang and Gillian said goodbye and dashed to the kitchen to answer.

"Hello?"

"Hello, Gillian? It's Caroline Everett. I hope I'm not catching you at a bad time."

"Not at all. How nice to hear from you."

"I just talked to Maud on the phone. She was so delighted to learn you were here. She wants to see you. Would you be up for a trip to Portland in a few days to visit her? She was Sophie's dearest friend."

"I would love to."

They arranged to go on Wednesday and then chatted briefly.

Gillian hung up, happy at the thought of spending time with women who had known her great-grandmother. She'd found several family albums, with pictures of a woman who had to be Sophie. Maybe she could take it so Caroline and Maud could confirm her suspicions.

Just after ten-thirty Monday morning, Gillian drove over to Joe's house. He came out the back door before she reached it. He was dressed in jeans and a pullover shirt. Somehow he'd shaved and he looked terrific.

The now-familiar racing of her heart began as soon as she saw him.

"Good morning," she said as she dashed around to open the passenger door for him.

"Good morning to you, too. Jenny wanted to come, but I told her it wasn't important enough to miss school."

"But it didn't hurt to ask," Gillian said with a small laugh. She remembered wanting to skip school a time or two.

The day was bright and sunny. The ocean sparkled in the distance as they drove into Rocky Point. Traffic was practically nonexistent. Such a change from the crowded streets and freeways of Las Vegas. The drivers that passed them lifted a hand in greeting, which Gillian was pleased to return. She loved this town.

"I don't know where the doctor's office is," she said when they reached the first intersection in town.

"Two more intersections, then hang a left. I'll call one of the men from the shop to take me home," he said.

"Why bother? I'm here, and I can shop while you're being seen to and then take you back." She turned where directed and saw the medical building, a low brick building with plenty of parking in front.

He managed to get out of the car unaided and leaned over to look at her. "Okay. Come back in about forty-five minutes. I'll wait out front if I get finished earlier." He hesitated a second. "I wanted to run by the shop as well."

"I'm at your service," she said.

She loved the idea of seeing where Joe worked. And the fire guns his daughter spoke about.

He grinned. "Then how about I buy us lunch at Marcie's and then give you the grand tour of the shop?"

"Sounds like a plan."

She wanted to say how very much she'd like it, but she didn't want to come across too eager. Watching him walk into the medical building, Gillian sighed. She was becoming far too interested in her neighbor.

When they entered the café shortly after noon, the place was crowded. Marcie was not to be seen, but one of the waitresses came over and smiled at Joe. "I have a table for you two, and Marcie asked me to let her know when you arrived. We've had a mess today. The espresso machine broke. Then the order was wrong from the bakery. Two people called in sick. Nothing like starting the week off with a bang," she said as she led the way to a small table near the back.

"I'll be right back to take your order," she said.

"It must be hard to run a place like this if problems spring up all the time," Gillian said, looking at the menu.

"Marcie's done well for herself. You should see this place in summer. She opens up the side patio to offer more tables. She often has people waiting for up to an hour."

"Hey, you two. How are the hands?" Marcie asked, giving first Joe a quick hug and then Gillian.

"Better."

He flexed them slightly. The bandages were pristine white and didn't seem as bulky.

"I can actually use the fingers of my left hand a bit without pain. Doc says it'll be a couple of more weeks, and then I have to take special care in day-to-day activities for a while."

"Good."

Marcie sat with them for a little while. Lunch passed swiftly, with Gillian enjoying the banter between Joe and Marcie, including Gillian when they could. From their conversation she could tell they'd grown up together and were good friends. She, too, had a couple of long-time friends from school. They got together whenever their busy schedules allowed. Here in Rocky Point, it'd be easier to maintain friendships as the pace of life was slower and no one ever seemed to be in too much of a hurry to stop and exchange greetings.

After lunch Gillian drove them over to Joe's shop. The huge warehouse sat on the edge of town near the water.

"It was used for storage before I bought it. It's perfectly situated for the ocean breeze, which helps keep it cool in summer," he said when she parked and eyed the structure curiously.

"Come in. I'll show you around," Joe said.

A large opening with the roll-up door high above them offered entry into the cavernous space. Three cars in various stages of restoration sat on blocks. Two men worked on one car, one on another. When they saw Joe, they quit what they were doing and came to greet him.

Gillian recognized Frank and said hello with a smile.

Joe quickly made introductions and then asked for an update. Going over each car, learning what had been done and what was next fascinated Gillian. She followed him around and listened attentively, bubbling with questions. This glimpse of Joe's work gave her new insights to the man. What patience he had to work on such detailed tasks. She could tell from his discussion with his employees that he didn't want to rush any step but gave each job individual attention.

The older cars were lovely. The long, sleek lines of the car in front had her thinking of the elegant days of the 1920s. When it was restored, she knew it'd be beautiful.

She looked around the huge space. There were lifts and hoists, an assortment of tools she could only guess at. Spare parts were neatly tagged along one wall, awaiting installation. One area had been slightly enclosed to form an office. There were two desks, a long counter stacked with papers and a couple of file cabinets.

Despite the activity on the cars, the huge warehouse was spotless. Joe obviously took great pride in his company and its work.

"I know you can't use your hands, boss," Toby said. "But could you give your opinion of the color match of the interior upholstery with the exterior paint we plan to use? We couldn't get the oatmeal color we wanted, but this is supposed to be close."

"Then I'd like to show you something," another man said.

Gillian was content to watch and learn as much as she could, but Joe turned to her. "Looks like I'll be here a while. Frank can run me home. Thanks for the ride to the doctor's."

"If you're sure. I don't mind waiting."

"No, you go on home. Thanks for the ride in."

"Thank you for lunch."

Since she was on her own again, she drove to the grocery store to stock up. Twenty minutes later she put her bags of groceries in the trunk and headed out of town. As the road made its big sweep around the bluffs she caught a glimpse of the sea as she drove toward home. Idly planning what to have for dinner that evening, she pressed the brake to slow for the sharp turn before climbing the slight hill to home.

Nothing happened.

Her foot sank to the floorboard.

She pumped the brakes, panic flaring.

The car wasn't slowing at all. She was going too fast to make the hairpin turn.

She tried the brakes again and again.

Time seemed to slow.

Everything jumped out at her in clear relief, the green of the ground beside the road, the black ribbon of asphalt turning sharply to the right. The scattered trees banking the road.

Holding on tightly, she tried to make the turn, but the car spun out and off the road, coming to rest in the soft soil when it slammed against a sapling.

Gillian caught her breath, her fingers gripping the steering wheel tightly. She closed her eyes and took a breath. Her heart pounded. For a moment she couldn't think.

"Thank You, Lord, for keeping me safe," she said aloud.

Slowly she released her grip.

She was okay.

She was fine.

She was scared to death!

"You all right?" An older man hurried across the short

distance from the road, peering in at her, the door to his car hanging open.

"I think so," she said, trying a smile, feeling her lips tremble.

She refused to give way to shock. She was okay.

She opened the door and stepped out. "My brakes didn't work," she said, looking at the car.

The front fender was crumpled slightly where it rested next to the small tree. Leaves and branches covered the windshield and hood of the car.

"Here, take it easy," he said, holding her arm gently. "You didn't hit your head or anything, right?"

"No. It seemed to happen in slow motion."

"It's a sharp turn. You were going too fast," he said.

"I tried to slow down, my brakes wouldn't work," she repeated.

"Come along. I'll run you into town. Maybe have someone at the clinic look you over to make sure you aren't hurt."

"I'm fine, really. I do appreciate your stopping. Let me get my purse."

Two others cars pulled to the side of the road. The driver of one called out, asking if they needed help.

"Call the sheriff when you can," the Good Samaritan called back, still at Gillian's side.

Both front doors of the second car opened and two tall men got out. As Joe ran across the grass, Gillian felt a wave of relief.

"Gillian, are you all right?" He pulled her into his arms

and hugged her gently. "What happened?"

"I'm okay. What are you doing here?" she said, relishing the safety she felt in Joe's embrace.

"Frank's giving me a ride home, remember?"

Frank caught up, and he looked concerned. "This is a sharp curve. Were you going too fast?"

From the comfort of Joe's arms, Gillian turned her head and explained what happened.

"I can take it from here, George," Joe told the older man standing beside them. "She's Sophie's great-granddaughter, living at the old house. I'll take her home."

"Okay, then. You take it easy for a day or two," he said kindly to Gillian.

She thanked him again and slowly stepped out of Joe's embrace.

"I bought groceries," she said. "I need to get them before we leave. And then call a tow truck, I guess?"

She looked at the car again. "I was so scared."

"I'll take care of the groceries," Frank said. "You go on over to my car and sit down."

Joe walked beside her. "Tell me again what exactly happened."

She explained again, and by the time they reached Frank's car, she was shaking with nerves.

Joe flung an arm around her shoulders and hugged her gently. "You're okay now. I don't understand how the brakes could fail on a new rental. We'll contact the company and let them know. They'll send someone out to check it over and bring you a new car."

"I think I want a Hummer next time. It happened so fast I was only afraid for a moment, but now when I think what might have happened if I hit one of the big trees head-on, I feel sick."

"But you didn't hit one. Your guardian angel was watching out for you today," Joe said, giving her another small hug.

She tried a smile. "I think you're right."

"You'll have to get the door," he said.

She opened both side doors then slid into the backseat, resting her head against the high cushion. "I'm so glad you were on your way home now."

"Me, too."

He frowned and looked at her car. "It could have been so much worse," he murmured.

Gillian knew he was remembering the car accident that killed his wife. She shivered.

It could have been far worse.

"I seemed to be jinxed. First the fire, now the car."

He was silent, and she opened her eyes to look at him. "What?"

"Nothing. Curious, that's all."

Frank returned with the two bags of groceries and put them beside Gillian. "I don't know if the car is drivable, but I left the ignition key under the floor mat. I think these are yours," he said, handing her the key ring.

"Thanks."

Gillian tried not to relive the moments of spinning out of control, but it was hard not to.

Frank insisted on carrying in her groceries when they

reached her house, and Joe went in with them.

"Thanks, Frank. I'll walk home from here," he said as the other man prepared to leave. "I'll walk you out."

"Okay. See ya, Gillian," he said.

Gillian put away the refrigerated items and was stowing the others in the cupboard when Joe returned and asked to use her phone.

"Hey, Tate, got a favor to ask. You hear about Gillian Parker's crash at the hairpin curve on the road out of town?…Yeah, well you're going to think I'm crazy, but can you let one of my guys look at the car?…Just a gut feeling. It's a fairly new car, and rental agencies always check them between rentals, so I'm surprised the brakes failed with no prior warning…No, just wanted to check…Thanks, I appreciate it."

Gillian leaned against the counter and watched him as he finished the conversation. "Who was that?" she asked when he'd hung up.

"The sheriff."

"And you want to examine that car because…?"

"Just a hunch."

"That it was tampered with?" she guessed.

He inclined his head slightly.

"Why would anyone tamper with my brakes? I don't have anyone mad at me that I know of. I hardly know anyone in Rocky Point. It doesn't make sense."

"No, it doesn't. I could be way off base. But it wouldn't hurt to check, would it?"

She shook her head. "I think I'll fix a cup of tea and sit

down," she said, feeling the after-effects of the adrenaline spike.

Joe watched her go through the ritual of preparing tea. He thought the actions were as important as the soothing effects of the beverage. She used loose tea the same as Sophie had.

Why hadn't Sophie ever contacted her?

Gillian offered him a cup which he accepted.

"I can only stay until the school bus comes," he said, glancing at his watch. "Then I have to be home for Jenny."

"We can have it out on the porch if you want," she said when the water boiled.

"Sounds good."

The porch needed work, as did the entire outside of the house. He wished Sophie had had the money to keep it up. Living in a similar home, he knew how much constant upkeep it demanded.

Still, he suspected Gillian was up to the challenge.

She sat in one of the Adirondack chairs and he sat in the other. Sipping the hot beverage, she looked pensive.

"I almost feel as if someone is trying to run me off," she said slowly. "That's what you're thinking, isn't it?"

"It's a possibility."

"And the only one who benefits is my father. But do you really think he'd try to kill me to get the land? If the house burned, he would have accomplished two things at once—getting rid of me and clearing the land for maximum sale value."

"I have a hard time picturing Robert setting fire to that pile of trash. Besides, a surer thing would have been setting fire to the house itself," Joe said. "He's older, so we never were friends, but as far as I know, he's more into charming himself into people's good graces than using force of any kind. And most fathers would never harm their children."

"Just abandon them," she murmured.

"Do you know the reasons?"

"To look for the pot of gold at the end of the rainbow."

"His loss."

She beamed at him. "What a nice thing to say."

"True."

He felt awkward giving out compliments. But that was the truth. He suspected she didn't hear enough genuine compliments.

Joe wondered how he could change that for her. She was not only beautiful on the outside, but she had an inner beauty that made her kind and loving. Jenny already adored her. If he were honest, he'd admit he was attracted to his new neighbor. Was he being foolish to try to resist?

Pamela's rejection had cut deep. Would he be able to open his heart to someone else? Someone like Gillian?

"I hope the events around here aren't putting you off Rocky Point," he said.

She turned her head to study him for a moment. "I lived a pretty routine life in Vegas. I worked as an aerobics instructor but could have done that in any town in the country. I have friends who like to ski together in winter and go to the movies or barbecue during the hot summer months. I taught Sunday School for the last seven years. And I sang in our choir. That gave me the most delight. Once I get settled, I plan to see where I can be useful at Trinity Church. So a few setbacks aren't going to change my feelings for Rocky Point or the people I've met so far."

It was hard to look beyond the glorious hair, bright blue eyes and porcelain skin. His biggest fear was she would get tired of the small town and want to return to Las Vegas.

But her words had his hopes rising.

Gillian looked over at his house. "I think you have a visitor," she said.

Joe looked and saw a car drive up and pull straight around to the back. A man got out. For a moment Joe thought he recognized his brother. But he knew he was imagining things. Zack was thousands of miles away, caught up in his own life, making a name for himself in the racing circuit, running from the past.

"When no one answers, he'll leave," Joe said.

"It could be someone from the church. Or your brother," Gillian said quietly.

Joe looked at her.

"What do you know about my brother?"

"Jenny had me e-mail him about you getting injured. She wanted him to come home to help out. It's what families do."

He sat up on the edge of the chair straining to see if the man was Zack. "I can't believe it. I think you're right. It is Zack."

"He's probably wondering where you are," she said.

He glanced at her as he rose. "You'll be okay?"

"I'll be fine. See you later."

Joe surprised them both by brushing his lips across her

cheek. "You take care of yourself." He turned and walked with a long stride across the grass to his house.

Gillian watched, covering her cheek with one hand, smiling at the tug of emotions. She was falling for her next door neighbor. And she hadn't a clue in the world if he was feeling anything beyond neighborliness toward her.

She sighed softly. Help me please, Father, to know what I should be doing here. I want to belong. I want to make friends and get a job and make a home. Is this the path You have for me? If not, could You please let me know? And, if it is Your will, please let me have a better understanding of Joe. He's so special. Thank You for bringing him into my life.

Wishing she could be there when Joe met his brother, she watched until he turned the corner of his house and disappeared from her view.

Nothing to do now but continue on. Nothing was certain—not her ownership of the house or her fitting in at Rocky Point. And most especially not her place in Joe's life.

Joe opened the door with only a minor twinge in his left hand. Stepping inside he immediately saw his brother leaning against the counter.

"Some things never change. This view for one," Zack said. He looked at Joe's hands and shook his head. "What happened? I heard about the fire, but not the details."

"Caught a burning board as it headed my way."

"Next time, duck," Zack said.

"If I had, it would have hit Gillian square in the face. A few burns on my hand are small exchange for something that could have been much worse. Besides, I've had burns before.

Painful, but they heal."

"Minor ones from an acetylene torch sparks. Not both hands at once."

"What are you doing here?" Joe asked. The question sounded harsh and ungrateful. He didn't mean for it to be. "I'm glad to see you, Zack," he added.

"Hey, Jenny and Gillian sent for me. I'm here to help."

His gaze was steady and genuine.

Joe studied the man he hadn't seen in years. Zack looked tired and thinner than the last time he'd seen him. Over six feet, he was still a tall, robust man, but the age showed on his face more than Joe had expected. Both were in their thirties now, though Zack was two years younger.

"You look wiped out," he said with brotherly candor.

Zack laughed and came across the room to give Joe a bear hug. "Always could count on you to be honest—no matter what."

Joe returned the embrace, thankful his brother was alive and home.

"Jenny will be delighted to see you," Joe said a moment later when Zack turned to straddle a kitchen chair.

"How old is she now? Five, six?"

"Seven."

Zack sighed. "I've been busy. Sorry I can't get back more often."

"You're doing well. We follow your races on the Internet," Joe said. "Want coffee or something?"

"Yeah, sure. Let me get it, though. You shouldn't be using those hands."

The kitchen was silent for the entire process of brewing the coffee. Zack kept his focus on the task at hand. Joe wondered what his brother had been doing for the last few years, beside racing. Did he have good friends, a relationship with a special woman?

Suddenly he thought of Marcie. She'd be shocked to know Zack was back. He had to call and let her know. It would be too unfair to have her bump into Zack in town with no warning.

He heard the sound of the school bus.

"Jenny's home," Joe said.

Zack poured both mugs full of coffee. "Can you hold this?"

"A straw would be better. I burned my mouth the first time I had coffee with a straw, but I'm better about it now."

Soon Jenny ran into the kitchen, bubbling with excitement. "Daddy, guess what—" She stopped abruptly when she spotted Zack leaning against the counter. Her eyes widened. She looked at her dad then back at Zack.

"Are you my uncle Zack?" she asked.

"I am. You've grown since the last time I saw you," he said

"I'm growing up. One day I'll be as tall as Aunt Marcie," she said proudly. "You got my e-mail didn't you? Gillian helped me write it." She beamed at her father. "We got him home to help."

"Good job, punkin'. Family needs to rally 'round in difficult times."

"And Gillian lives at Sophie's house. She's my friend.

She's really tall and dances. Daddy, can I learn to dance?"

"You dance around the house just fine," Joe said.

"But not air-robecks."

"Air robecks?" Zack repeated.

"I think you mean aerobics," Joe said, remembering what Gillian did for a living. Which probably accounted for her terrific figure. And her graceful walk.

"So, can I?"

"We'll see," Joe said.

"That means no. I can't do *anything*," she said to Zack.

"What else do you want to do that you can't?"

Joe watched the puzzled look on Zack's face. He'd learn soon enough that Jenny's conversations jumped around like crazy.

"I want a bike. But Daddy says no. And a pony, but even Gillian said that was far down on a pri-ty list. I can't even go roller-skating with Rachel 'cause it's too dangerous." She threw her father a dark look, hefted her backpack and walked out of the room. They could hear her footsteps on the stairs. All enthusiasm gone.

"Roller-skating's dangerous these days?" Zack asked.

Joe took a deep breath. "Leave it alone, Zack. You forfeited your right to give advice when you left."

"I'm here now," he said, "and I plan to stay long enough to build bridges back to where we used to be."

Chapter Seven

"So tell me about this Gillian. From what you said, you saved her from getting burned. She's tall and teaches aerobics. And lives next door? Related to Sophie?" Zack resumed his place on the turned-around chair, placing his mug on the table.

"Sophie died a couple of weeks ago. Gillian's her heir. Maybe."

Zack looked surprised. "I didn't know. I can't imagine home without Sophie next door."

"She was in her nineties. Slowing down a bit, but still strong about some things. I miss her, and so does Jenny. Though I think Gillian's making up for Sophie's being gone."

Zack finished his coffee. "I'm here for a few weeks. Let me know what I can do to help."

"People from the church have been helping out," Joe said. "And Gillian."

Zack nodded. "Good. I remember the church rallying around whenever someone needed help. And how they helped us out when Mom and Dad died."

"It's a blessing to be part of God's family," Joe said. He wondered if Zack still attended church. He hadn't gone the last time he'd visited.

Zack put his cup in the sink and headed for the back door. "I'll get my things from the car."

"Take the room at the back of the hall. The bed needs sheets."

"Got it."

The house had been their family home growing up. When their parents died, it went to Joe as the oldest son. But Joe hoped his brother knew he always had a home here.

The phone rang, and Joe picked it up without thinking, wincing at the pull on his burned palms.

"Kincaid," he said.

"Joe, it's Tate. We had one of your men look at the car. The brake line was tampered with. I'd say someone sabotaged the car. Puts the accident in a whole new light. If she'd been somewhere else with the brakes failing, well, I don't need to tell you about what could have happened."

Joe closed his eyes. Pamela's brakes had worked and the car crash had still been devastating. There were curves that had no trees around them, some of which could lead straight to the sea. He gave a quick prayer of thanks to the Lord for watching over Gillian.

"So where do we go from here?" he asked the sheriff.

"I'm asking around town to see if anyone saw someone hanging around her car today. Don't know exactly when it happened, but the puncture leaked brake fluid. Once we knew to look for it, we found traces in front of your shop, at the market parking lot and some dribble on the road before the accident scene. Do you know of anyone who would want to harm our new town resident?"

"I don't. I asked her and she said she couldn't think of anyone. Except maybe her father. But that doesn't sound like something Robert Parker would do."

"I'll keep looking. I also plan to talk to the fire inspector again about that fire at her place. It's starting to seem someone has targeted that young lady."

"I hope not." Joe made a silent vow to keep an eye on Gillian, to make sure nothing else happened to her.

Caroline Everette arrived at eight Wednesday morning, and in no time the two of them were driving to Portland.

"Maud's so happy you're coming," Caroline said as she merged with light traffic on the highway. "I talked to her twice yesterday. She had me run by her home and pick up some things for her. Breaking a hip is usually very bad for a woman her age, but her doctor said she would make a complete recovery."

"I'm looking forward to meeting her. You said earlier she actually went to school with my great-grandmother."

"Oh, they started first grade together. That was in the days before kindergarten. Our school isn't large, even today, so they were in the same classes all along. I didn't meet Sophie until I married James and moved to Rocky Point. That was about fifty years ago."

"So you knew her a long time. Tell me more about her."

Caroline smiled and started right in with, "Sophie was a pistol. She had a sense of humor that kept us in stitches every time we saw each other. And she had a way with flowers. I noticed the gardens when I drove in. She won prizes at the county fair for her roses, you know."

"I do know. Marvin Henny stopped by. He'll be taking care of things from now on."

"Good. Marvin is honest as the day is long and he has a way with plants."

Caroline continued reminiscing for the remainder of the trip. Gillian listened, enthralled. Once she discovered she had so much in common with Sophie, she wished more than ever that they'd met.

The rehab center was larger than Gillian expected. Built of brick, all on one level, it had two long wings that branched from the main portion of the building.

They met Maud in the sunny social hall. She was in a wheelchair. Her thinning white hair was done up and her makeup was perfect for a woman in her nineties. She beamed at Gillian as she and Caroline crossed the room to greet her.

"You look a lot like Sophie—though you're taller. Or does that just seem so because I'm in this chair?"

"She's much taller than Sophie," Caroline said, giving her friend a kiss on the cheek. "Here are the things you requested. Including Sophie's darling Gillian."

"Sit, sit. I'm so delighted to meet you, Gillian. Sophie told me all about you. Tell me, how do you like Rocky Point?"

"I love it."

"Settling in okay?"

Gillian nodded. "I went to church last Sunday and met so many people. And I've been exploring the town. One shopkeeper—is it Betsy Murphy?—offered a discount at her fabric store if and when I want to do up new window coverings, and she gave me the name of someone to sew them. Marcie Evans has been very friendly. And of course I was happy to meet Mrs. Everett," she said with a smile at the older woman.

"Call me Caroline, dear. I'm not that old yet!"

Gillian smiled. The woman had to be in her late eighties, if not older. "Thank you, I will, Caroline."

"And I'm Maud. I was Sophie's best friend." For a moment the sparkle left her eyes and she looked sad. "I miss her. We shared a lot during life's journey. Well, it won't be too long before I see her again."

"Now, Maud, you know the doctor said you'll be good as new before long."

"I am ninety-three, Caroline."

Caroline patted her hand. "Stay around long enough to help Gillian get settled."

Maud laughed. "That I'll do. Hand me that envelope I asked for, please."

Caroline placed it in her hands.

"There's something in here for you, Gillian," she said, as she rummaged around the thick packet. Pulling out an envelope triumphantly, she waved it in the air for a moment. "From Sophie." She handed it to Gillian.

Gillian looked at it.

"Go on and open it. I was supposed to give it to you if you showed up for the funeral, but this broken hip made me miss it. Caroline gave me a full report, but I wish I could have been there. Read it."

"Maybe we should give her some privacy," Caroline suggested.

"Oh, very well. Push me over by the window, will you. You can give me some more details about the funeral."

Gillian slid her finger beneath the flap, breaking the seal, and withdrew two sheets of paper.

Dearest Gillian,

My biggest regret in life is not having met you in person. I hope by leaving you my estate, such as it is, it will make up for that. I was thrilled when Robert told me he and his wife were expecting a baby. I thought at the time it would be a bridge to heal the gap between us. He had been such a sweet boy. I think losing his father so young, and being raised by his mother, had a lasting effect that was not always the best. Still, he is my grandson and I hoped to recapture the family ties we had once enjoyed.

He wanted me to give them money to help with the baby expenses, he said. A lot of money! That was not something I could do. Imagine my dismay when he returned a scathing letter saying he wanted nothing to do with me and that he'd take steps to make sure I never bothered him or his family again. I tried calling and writing to no avail.

My friend Maud said to wait until the initial anger had worn off before trying again. Periodically over the years I'd write. My letters were returned. He never changed his mind.

I know when he left you and his wife. I wrote immediately to her offering to have you both come to Maine. I didn't have a lot of money, but I had my house. She refused. I have no idea what tales he told about me, but she was as adamant about severing ties as he had been. I don't know what you think of me, but I will continue in hope that you will come to learn the truth in the future .I've lived a long life. It hasn't always been happy. My one bright joy in recent years was learning how well you were doing. I honored your parents' request not to contact you, but now I'm beyond their censure. I hope you will give Rocky Point a chance. It's been a wonderful place to live, and the house has been in our family for generations.

There are no restrictions, however. My estate is yours to do with what you will. But please know always that I would have loved you, and only sought the best for you. Fondly, Sophie Parker

Gillian sat silently for a long time. Her father had kept her from knowing this warm, loving woman. How could he have severed ties so completely? She felt the yearning behind the words. The painful acceptance that she not contact Gillian. Sadness and anger mixed as she thought about the entire situation.

"How dare he," she said in a quiet voice. Family was much more important than money. How could he have turned his back on his own grandmother—especially if, as she said, they'd once been close?

She looked up at the two elderly women waiting by the windows. They watched her quietly.

Rising, she crossed over to them and handed Maud the letter. She might already know of its contents, but she had been her great-grandmother's friend. Maybe she could shed more light.

"She knew all about me from detective reports," Gillian said, pulling a straight chair over to sit on. "I found them in her desk."

"She never stopped hoping somehow you'd find her. From what Caroline says, you never even knew she was alive."

"Not a clue. I was stunned when I got a call from Julian Greene telling me of my inheritance. Which is being challenged by my father."

"No!" the two echoed simultaneously.

"Foolish old women often hope the future will be different from the past. About eight or ten years ago Robert came to visit. He stayed three weeks and almost got away with taking her life savings when he left. Fortunately Sophie wasn't quite as gullible as he thought."

"He gave Julian Greene a will dated two years ago, written in Boston, saying she left him the house," Gillian said.

"Nonsense!" Maud said vehemently. "She had his number. Besides, she gave me this letter only last year. Obviously she means for you to have the house."

Gillian took it back and scanned it quickly. "There's no date on this."

"I can tell Julian about it, when she gave it to me," Maud said.

"We both can tell him of the regret she had for the family breach. She blamed Robert's mother. She was a greedy woman."

"Now, Caroline, don't speak ill of the dead."

"It's not speaking ill if it's true."

"I wish I had known her. Why didn't she contact me once I was grown? Or when my mother died?" Gillian tried hard to understand.

"By then so many years had gone by. I think she felt she had to honor your parents' wishes, no matter how much she disliked them," Maud said.

"Now it's too late."

"Well, you've got us. We can tell you all about Sophie, from when she first tried smoking back in Farmer Elias's back field when we were eight, to the time she beat all the town elders at horseshoes," Maud said.

"And how she made the best red velvet cake," Caroline said. "Remember? My, I love that cake."

Sophie's long-time friends filled the afternoon with stories that had Gillian both laughing and in tears. Gradually she was coming to know the woman and regret hit even sharper that they'd never met.

"It's getting late. We have to be going," Caroline finally said.

"Hmm. I'll be home in a couple of weeks. In time for Decoration Day anyway," Maud said.

"Decoration Day?" Gillian asked.

"Most folks call it Memorial Day. But for those of us who remember way back when, it'll always be Decoration Day."

"Oh, I can hardly wait. It's one of my favorite holidays," Caroline said.

"We have a festival at the church," Maud said.

"Maybe Gillian can help out this year. Sophie always made cakes and cookies. Do you bake?"

"I do. What else is involved? Are there booths and games for the children? At our church festivals, I ran the face-painting booth."

"Oh, that sounds like fun. Children love to have their faces painted. Didn't Mary Jane Williams do that several years ago?" Caroline asked.

"She did. Too bad she moved to Portland. Though I will say, she's come by to visit me a couple of times. We'd love to have you on the committee. I'll call Esther right away and let her know," Maud said.

"Sounds like fun." Gillian gave the woman a hug. "Thank you so much for all you've shared with me. I would have loved my great-grandmother."

Maud hugged her and smiled. "Sophie already loved you. She'd be so proud of you. Come see me again—maybe when I get back home."

"Okay. You heal fast. I'll add you to my prayers."

"Always knew you'd be like Sophie. Those reports showed us that long ago. Run along now. Thank you for coming," Maud said with a hint of tears in her eyes.

Caroline dropped Gillian at her door some time later and then sped off.

Once Gillian changed, she went to prepare something for supper. She called Joe to see if he wanted her to make enough for them.

"I'll be right there," he said.

Five minutes later he knocked on the kitchen door. Gillian opened it and smiled, her heart skipping a beat and then almost racing.

"How was your day?" Joe asked, stepping in.

"Terrific. I spent most of it with Caroline Everett and Maud Stevens. They told me so much about Sophie. Now I'm starting dinner. Can I fix enough for you and Jenny?"

"My brother, Zack, is visiting," Joe said.

"So it *was* your brother you saw Monday?"

"It was. He got your e-mail and hurried home. That surprised me. It's the first time he's been home in ages. He didn't even come back for Pamela's funeral."

"Maybe he was tied up at that moment and couldn't."

"Apparently my being injured overcame any other claims or reservations."

"Reservations?" she asked curiously.

He hesitated a moment, "It's not a secret. He left Marcie standing at the altar ten years ago."

"Literally?" she asked, looking shocked.

"Just about. Called the night before the ceremony. Marcie had a beautiful dress, the church decorated, the reception planned. Everyone at church was chipping in with food and cake and all. Everything was prepared. Hours before the ceremony, Zack took off, calling Marcie to say he had to leave. She was nineteen at the time. He was twenty-one and should have known better."

"If their love wasn't strong enough, better to part before the wedding than afterward, don't you think?" Gillian asked. She felt a pang of sympathy for a young Marcie who had probably been astonished her bridegroom left hours before they were to be wed. And heartbroken.

"It was the lure of car racing that drew him away. I know

he realizes he handled it badly by the way he never comes to visit—or only comes in time of emergency and then stays away from the town."

"How sad," Gillian said pensively. She remembered how her mother longed for her father after he left.

She had not seen that kind of longing in Marcie. Her new friend had moved on and didn't seem to suffer today because of the wedding that hadn't taken place.

"Water under the bridge. How are you feeling after the car crash?" he asked.

"I'm a bit stiff, mostly in my neck. It's better today."

"Let me know if you need anything."

She smiled. "Role reversal. Though with your new helper, I guess you won't be needing my help anymore."

He hesitated. "Actually, if you were to cook a nice, hot meal, I wouldn't turn it down. Unless things have drastically changed with Zack, he can't cook worth beans. Well, last night we had beans and franks."

Gillian nodded, pleased he'd asked. She still wanted to pay him back for helping with the fire. Plus she liked sharing meals with others. It was lonely to cook only for one. She often had friends over for dinner to give herself the opportunity to cook more than dinner for one.

"Deal. I'll make a quick stew for dinner and bring it over around seven."

She also was eclectic in her dishes, loving the hot, spicy Mexican food as well as the traditional dinners her mother had taught her. Experimenting with other ethnic fare was more fun and relaxing than a day at a spa.

She began blending the ingredients for the stew as soon as Joe left. The task relaxed her and freed her mind to think.

She wondered how Marcie had coped with her fiancé fleeing and leaving her to deal with the town that expected a wedding. Even though she'd only been in Rocky Point a short while, she knew the congregation at Trinity had been loving and kind in dealing with a canceled wedding. She could imagine the women she'd met on Sunday ten years ago. They would have tried their best to ease the heartache the young woman had experienced.

What kind of man was Zack Kincaid? Probably nothing like his brother. Joe interested her more than anyone. He was patient and kind. He'd saved her and then made it sound like no big deal. He was stoic with his burns, which she knew had to be extremely painful.

And he adored his little girl.

She wished she knew the full story about his marriage and its ending. He was blessed that Jenny wasn't severely injured. She was a delightful child. Gillian enjoyed her company.

When teaching Sunday School in Las Vegas, she had loved the children of that age, their wonder and delight in learning about the Lord. If an opening came up at Trinity for a Sunday School teacher, she'd apply. She hoped the new teacher of her former class loved her kids as much as she did.

Father, it's Your will I wish to follow. If I'm not meant to have the house, so be it. At least I've made some friends and could still stay in Rocky Point. These are wonderful people, a community that sticks together. I'd love to belong to a place like this. I await Your direction.

Just before seven, Gillian carried the pot of stew across

the grass to the house next door. She had a tote of warm rolls dangling from her arm. Jenny threw open the kitchen door before she reached the porch.

"Daddy said you were coming, so I was watching," she said, dancing in delight. "I'm so glad you cooked our dinner."

Lowering her voice and leaning closer, she said, "All Uncle Zack wants is hot dogs."

"You don't like hot dogs?" Gillian teased, stepping inside and noticing the kitchen table was already set with four places.

She placed the hot pot on the stove and the tote on the counter.

"Of course I do. But I like your cooking better," she said. "Oh, rolls. I love rolls!"

Joe came in, followed a moment later by Zack. Introductions were made in short order, and before long they were seated at the table, the savory stew filling the air with tantalizing aromas.

"I'll say grace," Joe said when Zack reached for the ladle.

His brother grimaced but withdrew his hand.

"Father, we thank You for the safe return of Zack. We thank You for keeping Gillian in your care when her car failed. Help us do Your will in all things and bring glory to Your name. Thank you for this food to the nourishment of our bodies and for this time of fellowship. Amen."

Zack looked at Joe and then Gillian, then reached out for the ladle, offering stew first to Gillian and then Jenny before filling Joe's plate and then his own.

He sat at a right angle from Joe, directly across from Gillian. It allowed him to help Joe eat with minimum fuss.

Gillian could tell Joe disliked the situation, but he accepted it with good grace.

"Uncle Zack races cars," Jenny said.

"So I heard," Gillian replied. Smiling at Zack, she tried to keep an open mind when she wanted to rail at him for hurting her friend so long ago. "NASCAR?" she asked.

"Grand Prix. Mostly in Europe."

"Wow, that sounds exciting."

Joe looked at her, then away. "Anything's more exciting than living in Rocky Point, I have that on good authority."

"Why, Daddy?" Jenny asked.

"Some people want more than friends and a sensible lifestyle."

"And some stay in the same place forever and do the same thing forever. Boring," Zack said.

"Or contentment. What's the Scripture Paul said about being content?"

Gillian answered, "One I know is from Philippians, chapter 4—'*I have learned to be content whatever the circumstances,*'" she quoted.

Joe looked at her in surprise. She smiled at him, her eyes dancing in amusement. She knew he was surprised. Did he continue to think because she had curly hair and blue eyes that she had no contact with God's Word?

"You must know the limitations of Rocky Point, Gillian," Zack said. "One movie theater in summer, closed in winter. Fish stories everywhere. Little to do or see."

"Yet we aren't far from Portland, if someone wants a crowded, big-city feel. Plus, it takes little for me to find contentment. I like my life," Joe said.

Zack laughed. "Portland is hardly on the same lines as Paris or Naples—or Las Vegas."

"Maybe not," Gillian spoke up, "but maybe some people are given different visions of what to do. God says *'For I know the plans I have for you, declares the LORD, plans to prosper you and not to harm you, plans to give you hope and a future.'* It's one of my favorite verses. Not everyone has the same plan laid out for them. And I expect there are different stages to every plan He has. I was born in Nevada. Now I find I have roots in Maine. I had nothing. Now I may have a house."

"I heard your father came up with a later will—leaving everything to him," Zack said.

"So it seems. That's still being investigated by people who knew my great-grandmother best. It doesn't seem in character for her. And sad as I am to say it, my earthly father doesn't seem to have the most stellar reputation. But I got a letter today from Maud, written by my great-grandmother. She wanted me to have the house. I can't wait to show Julian."

"What does it say?" Joe asked.

"I can show you later. She talks about why she knew about me but never contacted me. I understand her reasoning, but it's not something I would have done. If I wanted to meet someone, I'd go meet them."

"Different generation," Joe said.

"Quite a different upbringing," Zack added. "Tradition-bound New Englander versus Las Vegas girl."

"Maybe. I definitely would have handled it differently. I will treasure the letter."

"This meal is truly delicious," Zack said. "It reminds me—" He stopped suddenly. "Thanks, Gillian for preparing this for us. As I'm sure you heard, cooking isn't my forte."

"I'm happy to do it."

"Because when you give food to sick people, you give food to Jesus," Jenny said.

"I'm glad to help neighbors," Gillian said, flicking a quick glance at Joe. "And I love to cook for more than one."

His eyes met hers and she felt butterflies in her stomach. This was silly. She was a grown woman. If she liked someone, well and good. But to feel as shy as a schoolgirl was unreal. Yet she couldn't help how she felt. She liked being with Joe.

"I heard you're cleaning up the old house," Zack said after a moment of looking at his brother and his neighbor. "That's why you have the pile of trash behind your house that caught fire, right?"

"Yes. I should have had it hauled away each day. Joe saved the house, to his own detriment. We still don't how the fire happened, but the fire captain didn't seem to think it was spontaneous combustion."

"Which leaves arson," Zack said.

Gillian blinked. She had never thought it deliberately set. Frowning, she looked at Joe. "Is that what he thinks?"

"Possibility. I expect he'll be reviewing his notes after your accident. Seems odd that two accidents that could have caused substantial injury happened in such a short time."

"Conspiracy theories." She laughed. "I'm not the type to inspire conspiracies."

"What conspir-cy?" Jenny asked.

"Something from thriller books and spy novels. Nothing to do with us," Gillian said. "Who is going to help me clean the dishes?"

"I will," Jenny pipped up.

"Good, we can have some girl talk while we work and leave the men to do whatever they like."

"Daddy usually likes to watch the news. That's boring," Jenny said, jumping up to clear her place. She came back and took Joe's plate and utensils. Then cleared her uncle's. Gillian cleared her own. She put the remaining stew in the refrigerator. "I think there's enough for you two for lunch tomorrow if you want it."

The men did not leave the table while Gillian and Jenny did the dishes. Conscious of Joe watching her every moment, Gillian felt self-conscious and awkward. The easy talk between her and Jenny soon surfaced, however, and she was able to act in a rational manner when every cell in her longed to turn and talk to him, hear his voice, enjoy the exciting feelings that grew every time they were together.

"So then Karen got this cat that her grandmother had before she died. It's a mean cat. If I had a kitten I'd want it to be nice."

"Maybe the cat's scared. Think how different everything is away from the woman she loved, in a strange home, loaded with children when she probably never had little children around before."

"Maybe. I still want my kitten to be nice."

"I'm sure it will be," Gillian said. "When are you getting a kitten?"

"Not now," Joe said.

Jenny frowned. "Daddy never lets me have anything. Jimmy Mitchell at school has a cat who had lots of kittens. He's giving them away. A kitten can't eat much, can it?"

"It's not the money. You're not old enough to have a pet," her father said.

Gillian didn't want to contradict Joe, but she still felt he was too overprotective of his daughter. How was Jenny going to grow and learn responsibility if she wasn't allowed to do anything?

"Maybe you can get a cat and let me come visit," Jenny said softly.

Gillian looked at her and made up her mind instantly. Maybe she'd see about getting a dog. She'd always wanted a dog as a child, but living in apartments had made that impractical. Now she had a huge yard and house. At least for the moment.

The phone rang. Gillian had just dried her hands and was closest to the phone.

"Shall I answer?" she asked.

Joe nodded.

"Hello?"

"Gillian?"

"Hi, Marcie," she said, recognizing the other woman's voice.

"How's Joe doing?"

"Doing better. Do you want to talk to him?"

"Not necessary. Things are hectic here. Just let him know I called."

"I will."

"You sound different," Marcie said.

"Umm, that's right."

"Can't talk?"

"Right."

"I'll call you at home later," Marcie said and rang off.

Gillian replaced the phone and turned, keeping her eyes on Joe. "She just wanted to make sure you're doing okay."

He nodded, looking at Zack a long moment.

"She doesn't know I'm here," Zack said.

"She will before long. Someone's bound to have seen you in town."

Zack shrugged. "I didn't come in through town. Don't plan to go. I'm here for you."

"What about church on Sunday? Aren't you going with us?" Jenny asked, trying to follow the conversation.

"We'll see," Zack said, rising. "I'll watch a little TV, catch up on the news. You don't need anything right now, do you?" he asked his brother.

Joe shook his head.

"I'll be going home," Gillian said after Zack left the kitchen.

"I'll walk you back," Joe said. "It's growing dark out."

"That would be nice. Thanks for your help, Jenny." Gillian gave her a quick kiss on her cheek. "Don't stay up late, now."

Gillian relished the fresh breeze blowing in from the ocean. The slight tang of salt was still a novelty. One day she knew she'd probably not notice it. But for now it pointed out how different things were in her life from all she'd known before.

"Thanks again for dinner. It was delicious," Joe said as

they walked side by side.

"Happy to do it. How is it with Zack home?"

"He's a help. We're able to talk a bit. He's touchy about some things, but I guess I am, too. You enjoyed meeting Maud?"

"Oh, I sure did." She told him briefly about their visit and some of the stories she'd learned about Sophie and more about the letter.

"Hmm, makes you wonder, doesn't it?" he said.

"About?"

"Why Robert thinks he can get away with a scam. Sophie wanted you to have that house."

"I think she did. I hope she did. But what if he does have a later will? She could have changed her mind."

"I don't think so. Sophie was a wise woman. She knew what kind of man her grandson had become. It's still a mystery to me why she didn't contact you but I think she knew she wanted you to have the house. And I'm glad she did."

"Here we are," she said when they reached her back door. It was dark enough to hide the scorched siding. She hoped the slight hint of smoke would vanish soon. "If you hadn't seen the fire, I could have been burnt to a crisp. I feel so badly you were injured helping me."

"I'm glad I was here. My left hand is almost healed. The other will be better soon enough."

"I thank God every day for your help," she said slowly.

"I thank God every day for your being here," he said softly in the dark.

Gillian felt him move closer and then block the dim illumination from the light Gillian had left on in the kitchen.

His lips touched hers gently.

"Good night, sweet Gillian."

"Good night," she whispered.

In an instant he was gone.

Waiting a moment, she turned and entered her house.

Joe headed to the cliff. He could see well enough with the starlight. Not getting too close to the edge in case he misjudged the distance, he stared across the dark water to Rocky Point. Lights shone from house windows. Streetlights outlined the path of the roads. The greatest clusters were near the water and the town square. He knew which restaurant was Marcie's. He knew where his shop was. He knew every inch of Rocky Point. And loved it all.

Could Gillian grow to love the place as much as he did?

Could she grow to love him?

Chapter Eight

Gillian was in the back bedroom going through a familiar aerobics exercise to pounding music. She loved the open windows letting the ocean breeze keep things cool as she moved to the music. She'd purposefully emptied furniture from this room to use as an exercise space. When the phone rang, she reached for the portable she'd recently acquired. It was Marcie.

"I'm inviting you to lunch," she said when Gillian answered. "I thought we could have a picnic by the docks. There are some tables in the park, and the day looks as if it's going to be gorgeous."

"I'd like that. What time?"

"After the lunch rush, if that's okay with you. Say one?"

"I'll be there. What can I bring?"

"Nothing. I'll have something from the café for us. Stake out a good table with a view of the boats and I'll meet you there."

"Done."

Gillian resumed her routine with a smile on her face. A break from the work she was doing would be appreciated. She'd finished clearing all the rooms, but she didn't want to put more into the house until she knew if it were to be hers or not. She had sketches and lists for each room. If the house became hers, she had big plans for bringing it back to life.

She continued her routine until it struck her. She didn't have a car. How was she going to get to town?

As if thinking about the situation caused the sheriff to remember her, he called.

"We've finished with the car," Sheriff Tate said. "Joe said his guys could repair it if the rental company gave the go-ahead. He's contacting them. I've finished the report. Far as I can tell, it's malicious mischief. I'm keeping an eye out for restless teenagers who have little to do. I'll let you know once we find out anything further."

"Thank you. I didn't know Joe repaired regular cars. I thought he only worked on vintage ones."

"That's his line of work. For you he made an exception. Once he gets the go-ahead from the insurance agency, it should be ready to drive in a day."

"In the meantime, I'm stuck here," she said, thinking aloud.

"If you're planning to stay in Rocky Point, Stan Bremmer has some cars on his lot. He's reliable, and Joe could always vet anything you're interested in," the sheriff suggested.

"Thanks, Sheriff, I'll give him a call." Then she hung up.

The big question—was she going to stay in town even if the house went to her father?

She liked Rocky Point. She liked the people she'd met. And she more than liked Joe and Jenny.

Yes, if she could find work somewhere, she could live in

Rocky Point. Her savings wouldn't last forever, so finding a job would become a top priority.

The third call of the day, coming minutes later, was from Joe.

"How are your hands?" she asked.

"Better each day. My left one is almost healed. But that's not why I called. It occurs to me you have no wheels. Can we take you anywhere today?"

"What do you know about Stan Bremmer?"

"Good man. Goes to our church. I've known him all my life. Want a ride down this morning?"

On the spur of the moment, she made up her mind. "Yes, I'd like that."

"How about in an hour?"

"That would be perfect, thank you."

She was humming as she hurried to shower and change. It was only because he was being neighborly, she reminded herself. None of the anticipation bubbling up inside had to do with actually seeing Joe.

When she was ready, she grabbed her purse and headed across the grounds to his house. No sense in his having to come over to her house.

She had almost reached the back door when Zack opened it for her.

"Good morning. I hear you're getting a new car today," he said as she stepped inside the kitchen.

"Might, if Stan Bremmer has something I like."

"Joe can tell you about the insides. I can tell you about handling," he offered.

"I'll take any help I can get. I have an old clunker in Vegas. It wouldn't make the trip cross-country."

Something else to do—sell her car. Close her apartment, arrange for things she wanted to be shipped. Get rid of the rest. The list went on and on.

She didn't want to go back to Las Vegas, but she had to in order to wind things up with her life there.

"Do you still have an apartment in Vegas?" he asked.

Gillian nodded. "My furniture and most of my clothes are still there. A friend's watching my apartment for me. I'm paid up through next month and wanted to take that time to see if I really wanted to move here for good."

"And do you?" Zack asked.

"Most definitely!"

"Good morning," Joe said, coming into the kitchen.

She turned and smiled when she saw him. He looked better and better each time she saw him.

"Hi. Thanks for the lift."

"Hey, I'm driving," Zack said.

"But I'm the one who offered."

Gillian giggled at the play between the two brothers. They sounded like the kids in her Sunday School class.

When they arrived at Stan's lot, Gillian was glad the two men were with her. She would have driven right past it. Nothing like the huge automobile lots in Vegas with lights all over the place—this looked like Stan's side yard, with cars parked in an orderly manner. There were only eleven cars. Probably not as much business in Rocky Point as in Las Vegas, she mused, climbing out and starting down the line.

Stan came out, greeted Joe and then exclaimed surprise when he saw Zack. They talked while Gillian wandered down the row, trying to picture herself in one of the cars. Almost at the end she found a powder-blue sedan she liked. She slid behind the wheel and checked out all the features. A moment later she looked up and saw Joe in front, talking with Stan.

She looked into the backseat and then got out. "I like this one."

"Great bargain. Mrs. McFarland owned it for two years. Of course she only drove to church and the market. And once a year to the cemetery to put flowers on old Harold's grave. She wanted something smaller. Not too many miles on this baby," Stan said, patting the hood affectionately.

Gillian looked at Joe. "What do you think?"

He nodded. "It's a good car. Pop the hood for me and I'll give it a quick scan."

She did and then went to stand beside him as he gingerly touched belts and different engine parts. Her shoulder brushed his as she peered in, trying to understand what he was seeing.

He looked at her, his face only inches from her own. Gillian noticed the deep brown color of his eyes. She could feel his breath brush against her cheeks. Her heart skipped a beat. She remembered the kiss last night. Her heart beat faster.

"So?" she asked breathlessly.

"We can take it to the shop and have one of the men give it a thorough checking, but it looks good. And in Rocky Point, we would have heard if it had been in a fender bender. I think it's a good deal."

She smiled and nodded. "Thank you."

By the time she met Marcie at the park, she was the proud owner of a powder-blue car. Stan was driving it to Joe's shop, where one of his employees would check it out. After lunch, it should be all hers. In the meantime, Zack had dropped her at the park and driven his brother to the shop.

Marcie arrived shortly after one, carrying a large canvas tote. As she unpacked everything—from a small tablecloth to real china plates to ice tea glasses—Gillian was reminded of a bottomless hat magicians used. More and more items came from the bag. Finally the food appeared. The po'boy sandwiches were made with sourdough rolls, thick and enticing. The slaw was fresh. There were even brownies for dessert.

"What a feast," Gillian said.

"I aim to please. We offer this as a takeout option for summer visitors. Lots of people like to picnic and want something special. I just heard this morning about your accident. Are you all right? You didn't say anything about it when I called."

"I'm fine. The car is a bit of a mess. I talked to the rental agency and they are going to have Joe repair it enough to drive back to Portland."

"Joe?"

"His crew, actually. Though he said this morning his left hand was almost healed."

"Let's say grace and eat. You have lots to tell me," Marcie said, reaching out to hold hands with Gillian.

"Thank you Father for the blessings of this day. For the fellowship

we share with You and each other. Bless the food to the nourishment of our bodies and the conversation to the nourishment of our souls. May we please You in all we do. Amen."

"Amen," Gillian echoed, giving her friend's hands a small squeeze before releasing.

"Tell all," Marcie said as they began to eat.

Gillian explained about the brakes failing, about the sheriff's report and about buying her new car.

"Good move," Marcie said with a smile. "Shows you're putting down roots. I'm glad. But a bit surprised. Look at you—you're beautiful, talented, come from the land of lights."

"Sin City, you mean. I loved my neighborhood and the people I worked with, but I really don't mind being away from Vegas. I do need a job, however. If I don't find something locally, I might have to commute to Portland."

"You taught aerobics, right? How much space do you need if you open a place of your own?"

Gillian thought about it for a moment. Open her own exercise studio?

Why not?

"A good-size room, lots of light, with a landlord who won't mind music."

"I know just the place. There's a vacant warehouse next to Joe's shop. It'd be perfect. It was renovated from an open warehouse to a store a couple of years ago, but the kitschy items sold there weren't appealing to most tourists, and no locals patronized the place. The owner was in it for the quick buck. He vacated it at the end of last summer and it's been empty since then."

That would be just the thing—open her own aerobics center.

"Would there be enough women who want to exercise, that's the question."

"Who knows until you try?"

"I'll pray about it," Gillian said thoughtfully. Was this the direction God wanted her to go?

They watched the boats at the marina bob on the water for a moment, then Gillian looked at Marcie.

"Zack drove me in," she said.

Marcie nodded, putting her sandwich back on the wrapping. She sighed softly and met Gillian's gaze.

"I don't know if anyone told you our history. It's not a secret—everyone in town in those days knows about it. He and I were sweethearts in high school. We got engaged after I graduated. Then the day before the wedding, he took off."

She looked out at the sparkling water. "I still have the dress. It was so beautiful. I was so happy. Then, poof! Life changed in a day."

"I'm so sorry," Gillian said.

"I was, too. Then. But it's worked out for the best. I have my business, my friends and family. Rocky Point is home and I love it. It was one thing Zack and I couldn't agree on. Had we married, I probably would have traipsed all over the globe with him. And I'm not like that. I love it here. I like knowing my family has been here since the Revolution. When I go to the cemetery, I can see generations who made Rocky Point what it is today. Zack always felt stifled here."

"He said he wasn't coming into town, but he drove Joe

and me in today," Gillian said.

"He's only been home once or twice since he left. And thankfully I didn't run into him. But life goes on. He got what he wanted, and I have most of what I wanted, so thanks be to God we didn't make a mistake. Did I tell you Sarah Jane Bitswell is pregnant? She's the one in charge of the second-grade Sunday School class. You said if there were an opening, you'd like to volunteer."

Recognizing the change of subject, Gillian nodded and smiled. "I would love the chance. How many are in the class?"

She drank in all the information Marcie gave her. She knew her ties to Sophie Parker had her accepted by the community more readily than most newcomers could expect after so short a time. Everything seemed to point to her staying.

She missed her own Sunday School class. She'd love to become more involved with Trinity Church and teach some of the children who attended.

When lunch finished, Gillian walked to the wharf area, paying attention to the shops and buildings. The area was in an older section of town and obviously had been lovingly renovated. She passed Joe's warehouse with its wide doors and saw the smaller building that had a discreet For Rent sign in the window on the lower level. Cupping her eyes against the glare, she peered into the space through the front window.. It was huge. Much larger than she needed. It had wooden floors, and the walls were painted and in good shape. There were a couple of doors in the rear. She wondered what they opened to.

"Sightseeing?" Joe asked, sneaking up on her.

She spun around. "No, looking for a space to rent. Do you know who owns this?"

He studied her for a moment. "I do, actually," he said. "Why rent here when you have a perfectly good house you're living in."

She glanced up. There was another set of windows above the space she'd been looking at. An apartment? "Not for living. I thought I'd see about renting some space to open an aerobics studio. Is there a loft apartment as well?"

He nodded.

"Good to know in case the ruling over the property doesn't go my way. So how much is the rent?"

"For?"

"Start with the ground floor. Can I see it?"

"Sure." He called into his shop and in a moment one of the men she recognized from her previous visit brought a key.

She took it and opened the front door. The space smelled a bit musty, but a thorough cleaning would freshen everything. She almost laughed aloud. She'd done nothing but clean since she arrived.

She walked around the space, wondering if she could have some of the area walled off for separate studios. She could decorate one for adults and one for children.

"How much?" she asked.

Joe named a figure that to Gillian sounded surprisingly low. She nodded, not letting him see her surprise. Was he making a special deal just for her?

"What's in here?" she asked, opening one of the back

doors. It was a large lavatory in some disrepair. The second opened to another. It was definitely newer and in a better state. "Hmm, his and her restrooms."

"Could be. I'll make you a deal. You stay for six months and I'll give you the seventh month free."

She suspected even more now that he was giving her a special price. "How much improvements are you willing to throw in?" she asked, trying to keep the excitement from her voice. The rent was low enough that she didn't have to calculate anything. She could easily swing it even if she had only a few clients during the first months. And a seventh-month bonus was wonderful.

"What are you thinking about?" he asked.

"A couple of walls to break up the space, some paint, and some repairs to the bathrooms. Maybe wire it for surround sound."

He glanced around. "We can discuss it. If you put in some hours, the price would be lower."

"Happy to. I can wield a mean hammer. And I love to paint. The fresh look of the walls when they are all finished is such a great feeling." She looked at Joe and smiled. "Sounds like we have a deal. Do I sign a year's lease?"

"Not necessary. Your word is good enough for me."

Gillian felt the heat crawl up her cheeks at his look. For a long moment they stared at each other. Was she imagining things, or was he beginning to care for her?

"You're not going to paint it neon-pink, are you?" he asked slowly, his eyes never leaving hers.

She laughed and came up to him. Pointing to his chest,

she shook her head. "When we're both old and gray, are you still going to think I'm some showgirl from Vegas? I'm going to paint in light pastels, for an uplifting feeling."

He caught her hand in his and held it for a second, then brought it to his lips for a quick kiss.

"Time will tell," he said, his voice husky with emotion.

Gillian was mesmerized, speechless.

He released her and she tried to gather a semblance of composure.

"Yes, it will." She looked around, flustered. "Lots to do. I think I'll stop by the hardware store and see what colors I like."

She felt flustered. She wished they could call a time-out like football games did to give her time to relish the affection. She felt cherished. He was growing more and more dear to her and sometimes she believed she was growing special to him as well. She wanted to savor the moment.

Joe looked at her. Gillian fascinated him. Her bubbling enthusiasm was contagious. He liked her laughter and the bright light in her eyes. He was courting disaster renting her this space. He'd see her every day when she arrived. She might even suggest riding down together to save gas. He'd hear her plans and get caught up even more with his pretty neighbor. He was already more involved than was safe for his heart.

Help me, oh, God. I'm attracted to Gillian and know it could end in heartache. What do I do?

The space had sat empty for months. He wasn't that sure an aerobics exercise studio would exactly flourish in their small town, but it had to be better than the get-rich-scheme the previous tenant had.

"So, new car, new business. Everything is going great," she said with optimism.

"Except for your father and the will." Joe turned away and looked around the space.

"Yes. Well, I leave that up to God. He has my life's plan in His hands. I'm just doing my best to follow His wishes. However He settles things, I consider coming here a blessing."

Joe was struck again by her faith. Pamela had gone to church, but he sometimes thought she missed the amazing joy the love in Christ brought. He was saddened again at her loss, and Jenny would forever miss the love of her mother. He missed not having a loving companion in life's journey. Would he ever trust another to share his life with?

"Thanks, Joe. You're my blessing for today," she said, stepping on tiptoes and brushing her lips across his cheek. "See you tomorrow."

She almost skipped as she left. He watched her go, bemused.

He headed back to the shop, the image of Gillian sitting opposite him at the breakfast table suddenly popping into mind.

For a moment he wanted that to become a reality. To share a life with someone so upbeat and pleased with life whatever the circumstances.

Zack was leaning under the hood of one of the cars when Joe returned. He and Paul were discussing the timing device. For a moment Joe remembered a hope he'd had years ago, that he and Zack could run the business together.

Both had loved cars from childhood. Joe had always wanted to know how they worked. He admired the elegant cars of old, with their sleek lines and sweeping grandeur. Zack had loved driving, speed and the limelight. Joe wished things had been different.

Zack looked up. "Finished?"

"Ready to head for home. Jenny will be getting off from school before long."

"I'm done here. Paul and I were discussing maximizing the speed ratio and getting a few more miles per hour out of her."

"I doubt the owner is looking for a speed machine. He's paying big bucks to restore it to the 1937 look, not to drive on some raceway."

"Hey, the capability for speed doesn't mean he has to push it."

"We'll stick to the original plan," Joe said.

He appreciated his brother's help, but Zack had always been more interested in speed and performance than the esthetics of the beautiful old cars. Joe wasn't promising grand prix speed, only to restore the vehicle to the best of his ability.

The phone was ringing when Gillian entered the kitchen. She ran to answer it, disappointed to hear her father's voice on the other end.

"How about I take you out to dinner tonight? I have a proposition to make," Robert said.

"Can't you just tell me over the phone?" she asked.

"I could, but I thought a father should take his daughter out to dinner once in a while," he countered. "We could talk about the past. You could catch me up on what you've been doing. How about we drive to Portland and eat at the Spinnaker," he said. "It had great seafood."

After their last confrontation, Gillian was a bit wary. But he sounded nonthreatening on the phone, and she would dearly love to learn more about him. Was he sincere in wanting to learn about her childhood?

"All right."

"I'll pick you up at six."

Gillian had only a very few things suitable for an evening out. One was the black suit she'd worn at Sophie's funeral. It would have to do. With a bit of jewelry and a bright scarf, she'd dress it up. It looked more businesslike than festive, but she felt it suited the evening.

Her father arrived promptly at six. "So tell me about your mother. She was special to me," he began as they reached the highway.

So special he left her and never contacted her again, Gillian thought. She drew a deep breath. Maybe he was trying to make amends. "She missed you after you left. She kept hoping you'd come back. You never did."

"Guilty as charged. The life there got too much. I needed fresh places to see, and she wanted to stay put. I should have come back. I missed most of your growing up. Did you do well in school?"

"I wasn't an honor student, but did well enough."

"Better than your old man, I bet."

"Tell me where you've been all these years," she said.

It didn't take much to get Robert talking. Gillian was fascinated at the way he could spin a tale. He told of working in San Francisco then moving to the bright lights of New York. A few years in Miami before heading to Paris had her visualizing all the events as if she were watching a movie.

He had the gift of storytelling. Too bad he couldn't have turned that to some good. Underlying each episode was the reality that he'd made money and lost it, always trying for the pot of gold at the foot of the rainbow.

If he had expended all that energy in steady work, he would have had a good career, a good family life. But it didn't sound as if he wanted that.

Which made it more difficult for Gillian to understand how they could be related. Those were her primary goals—always serving the Lord to the best of her ability. She felt led to Rocky Point. Was she also chasing after an unattainable dream by wanting to set down roots and become a contributing member of the community? She didn't think so.

When they reached the restaurant, it was far more elegant than Gillian had expected. The meal was sumptuous. She was halfway through when she felt the atmosphere change slightly. Robert focused his gaze on her.

"The real reason I wanted to talk to you tonight is to offer to let you buy me out of the house. The longer I stay in Rocky Point, the more it drives me crazy. I'll sell you the house at a price less than market value."

Gillian put down her fork. "What makes you think the house is yours to sell?"

She hadn't told him about the letter Sophie had written. The lawyer, Julian, had been delighted to see it, even without a date. He'd even called and talked to Maud about when she'd received it.

"I have the later will," he said with confidence. He was too convinced he had the winning hand for it to be a scam.

She loved the house, but now it looked as if she'd been a bit premature. What if Robert had a later will. Something like that couldn't be faked—not if a reputable attorney had prepared it.

Wait.

It was as if a voice spoke directly to her.

She had the letter.

She smiled and picked up her fork. "I'll wait for the final determination, thank you," she said.

His sudden anger was evident, though he tried to control it. "I may not be so generous by then. This could take weeks, months to resolve."

"I can wait."

"You won't get this offer once the house is mine."

"Then maybe I should look elsewhere to live," she said easily. She would not be intimidated.

He frowned and began eating again. Conversation ceased.

Gillian grew uncomfortable with the silence.

"Why did you leave us," she asked slowly. "Was it because of me?"

He hesitated a moment before replying, then said, "I

wasn't ready for the responsibility of a family. By the time you were in school, I needed freedom."

She'd known it all along. But it hurt to hear the words. If she hadn't been born, would her mother have followed him on his travels?

"I've tried to be nice about the house. But if you are standing firm, I'm afraid it'll get messy. When I take possession, I won't be so ready to cut a deal. It'll go to the highest bidder," he said.

Gillian wondered what he considered being nice. She resented his trampling on her dreams.

"*If* you take possession. The judge let me live there until it's all settled, so it sounds like it is more likely to be awarded to me."

She was tempted to tell him about Sophie's letter but resisted.

"Small-town favors. The Boston attorney will know all the legal angles to play. If you'll excuse me?" He rose and headed toward the back and the restrooms.

Gillian finished her meal in peace, secretly relieved he'd left for the moment. Dinner was not turning out as she'd expected. Sipping her iced tea, she wished he hadn't brought up the house.

Was that the only reason he called her? To try to talk her in to giving him money?

Earlier, she might have given in—but now that she had Sophie's letter, she was content to wait. Why would Sophie leave it to her only to later leave it to her father? It didn't make sense.

But it did make sense that he would try to get money, if all the stories she'd heard about him were true.

As the moments ticked by, Gillian grew uneasy. Where was her father?

She summoned a waiter. "My father went to use the restroom some time ago. Can someone check to see if he's all right? Maybe he became ill."

The waiter returned in two minutes. "Sorry, miss, there is no one in the men's room."

Chapter Nine

Stranded.

For a moment, Gillian couldn't believe it. Maybe her father had gone out to the car to get something.

As the seconds ticked by, however, she knew he wasn't coming back.

Not only had he stranded her, but when the waiter discreetly delivered the bill, she knew Robert had stuck her with the check.

Anger flared. She'd made a good-faith effort to get to know him.

Now she was angry she'd been duped. And disappointed.

Everyone wanted a father who loved and cared for them. As her heavenly Father did.

For a moment she gave a brief thank-you prayer for all aspects of the evening. She'd gotten to know her father a bit better. Just because he'd ended up leaving her alone in Portland didn't negate the information she'd gleaned.

And it also proved the point Joe tried to make: Don't trust Robert Parker.

If only they'd eaten in Rocky Point, it would be easy enough to get home. Now, she was almost an hour away from town and doubted very much there was a taxi service that ran between here and there.

She paid the bill, thankful it wasn't exorbitant. When she reached the lobby of the restaurant, she asked the maitre d' if he knew about bus service between Portland and Rocky Point. He did not, but he offered to call a cab for her. Gillian went instead to the side of the lobby to call the bus company. If there were no buses running, she had to come up with another idea.

As it turned out, there was a twice-daily bus trip to Rocky Point, and the last bus had left hours ago.

Anger rose again. How dare her father desert her like that! She debated what to do. Finally she called Joe.

"Hello?" Zack answered.

"Hello, Zack. It's Gillian. Is Joe there?"

"Hold on."

In only a couple of seconds Gillian heard his deep voice.

"What can I do for you?"

"I need a ride."

"New car break down already?" he joked.

"No. I don't have my car and I have no way home. The bus doesn't run again until morning."

"Where are you?"

"Portland. My father brought me here for dinner then skipped out."

"Say no more. If you need a ride, I'm your man. Where exactly are you?"

She gave the name of the restaurant. He knew it and said he'd be there as soon as possible.

It was only after he hung up that she realized he couldn't drive, so Zack would probably be coming. She wished she hadn't had to bother them, but she did not want to stay away from the house knowing her father probably wouldn't hesitate to use any means to get his way.

A little over an hour later, Joe Kincaid strode into the restaurant's lobby where Gillian was sitting. She spotted him and rose, almost running to him. "Thank you for coming. I'm so mad at myself for getting in this situation. Did Zack drive?"

"Nope." He raised his left hand. Flexing the fingers, he smiled. "Almost as good as new. I managed. Come on. You can tell me what happened on the way back. You okay?"

She nodded. "Yes, but feeling rather foolish. Where's Jenny?"

"Zack stayed with her. We'll be home in an hour."

"Want me to drive?" she asked, conscious about the effort driving with injured hands must cause.

"Nope. I'm good to go."

Once they reached the highway, Joe glanced at her for a second and asked, "So, what happened?"

"My father invited me out to dinner. I believed it was a chance to talk about our family. Turns out he wanted to make a deal by letting me buy Sophie's house from him before he put it on the market."

"You didn't agree, did you?" Joe asked quickly.

"Of course not. You know about the letter. I think now it's all a scam—just like you suggested. I said I'd wait for the decision of the probate judge. I think that made him angry, so he took off. I'm so mad I could spit nickels!"

"I don't blame you," he said.

"And he stuck me with the bill, no less."

Joe laughed. "The man has guts, I'll give him that."

"It's not funny," she said.

"I think he's desperate and running out of time," Joe said thoughtfully. "Somehow he's not as confident as he'd like us to believe that it's a done deal. Maybe he didn't expect opposition."

"Or he's so impatient hanging around Rocky Point and wants to be gone."

"Never liked to stay in one place for long, the way I hear it."

"I'm going to give up trying to know him," she said.

"A man's actions speak louder than words. You know as much about him as you need to. Let it go."

"Let what go?"

"The dream of a happy family with a doting father. Let it go, Gillian." His voice was tender.

Gillian knew Joe was right. Still, the longing didn't completely vanish.

"You're right." She took a deep breath. "I have so much, and he has so little. I think I feel sorry for him."

"Good."

"Good?"

"You are grounded in faith. You have lots of friends where you lived in Vegas and here in Rocky Point. You have a good life. He has nothing."

She thought about that for a while. "It is sad, isn't it."

"It's also his choice," Joe said gently.

She nodded and fell silent. Staring out at the darkness, she wondered why one father would desert his only child, while another cared so much for His.

"I could walk to the front door safely on my own," she said once they reached her house and Joe got out of the car.

"My mother raised me right," he said, teasing her.

"Want to come in for a cup of hot chocolate? It's too late for coffee."

"I'd like that."

Gillian opened the door and started down the hall. When they reached the kitchen, she said, "Have a seat."

Joe sat at the old wooden table. He remembered Sophie bustling around her kitchen. She hadn't been as tall as Gillian. The last years she'd been thin, her long white hair worn in a bun. Had she been lonely living for so many years by herself in this rambling house?

"Did I tell you I may be teaching Sunday School at Trinity starting next week?" Gillian asked.

"No. When did that happen?"

"I'm still waiting to hear for sure, but the current teacher is soon to deliver a new baby and wants time off. So I asked to be considered. Pastor John is checking with my church in Nevada, but said I was practically guaranteed the spot. It's probably temporary until Sarah Jane wants to return. But I'll be able to teach for a few months at least. It's second-grade level, so I'll have Jenny in my class."

"She'll love that. I remember you said you taught Sunday School."

"It's so much fun with young children. They are so eager to learn everything."

Gillian poured the hot chocolate into mugs and set them on the table, taking the chair opposite Joe.

"Thanks again for coming to get me."

"My pleasure. I would like a few minutes alone with your dad, however."

She grinned. "To read him the riot act?"

"Umm, something like that."

"So tell me about your wife," she said out of the blue.

He was startled at the change of topic but figured Gillian had a right to know, if his instincts about her and her feelings were correct.

"Pamela and I went to school together. I went off to college while she stayed in Rocky Point, working at an insurance agency. When I got back, we got married then had Jenny."

"But something went wrong," Gillian guessed.

"She was restless living in Rocky Point. She wanted to experience life, as she said. Because I'd been to Boston for college, she constantly complained I'd gotten out and she'd never had a chance. She wanted to live in a big city for a while. Maybe I should have gone along with it, but after Jenny was born, I wanted to stay in town, not raise a child in the city. The more I protested, the more Pamela insisted."

He hated thinking about all the arguments and tempers

that had flared. The coolness with which Pamela treated first him and then Jenny still disturbed him.

Taking a sip of the chocolate, he replaced the mug on the table and stared at it. "The end came suddenly. I returned from work early one afternoon, thinking to take them to dinner at the café, but she was gone. Had I not come home early, I wouldn't have known for hours. But I headed out after her and came upon the wreck on the highway, about fifty miles south of here." He closed his eyes for a moment.

"Pamela had died at the scene. Jenny was airlifted to the hospital. She was in a coma for two days. It was touch and go. I've never prayed so much in my life. God heard me and she recovered completely. I'm forever grateful."

"Still, what a tragedy. I'm so sorry," Gillian said softly, reaching out to touch his wrist above the bandages.

"It wouldn't have been so bad if she hadn't taken our daughter. No, that sounds wrong. It *was* bad. But to put Jenny in danger was unconscionable."

"I'm sure Pamela never considered she wouldn't end up where she wanted to be. She didn't plan on an accident."

"I should have listened to her—really heard her. But I thought it was a phase. I thought she'd be caught up with motherhood and find happiness in that, but the older she grew, the more she felt she'd missed out."

"Sometimes it's true. People should have some life experiences before becoming part of a couple. And some couples are not meant to be. Look at my father and mother."

Joe suddenly felt drained. "It's late. I need to go," he said, not wanting to move, but knowing he needed to. It was pleasant in her kitchen—even talking over painful events from the past didn't hurt as much.

He was comfortable around her.

No, that wasn't the right word. He never quite knew what she was going to say next. At ease, but very interested, as well. Even as late as it was, she looked fresh and pretty and he hated to leave.

"Thank you again for coming for me. What can I do to repay the favor?"

"Want to pick up Jenny in the morning? She's at Sally Anne Robinson's, on Water Street. I can give you the address. It'll keep Zack from town and give Jenny some time to see you."

"Is he still avoiding Marcie?" she asked.

"So it appears."

"I'm happy to pick up Jenny. What time and where, exactly?"

After he gave her the address, he rose. "Thanks for the hot chocolate."

"Now I can walk you to the door," she said with a mischievous smile.

He nodded, heading for the front door instead of the few steps to the back door. It would give him a little longer with her. Oh, man, he had it bad.

"Maybe you'll let Jenny come over and bake chocolate chip cookies with me tomorrow when she gets home?" she asked tentatively at the door.

"Only if we get to share in some of the results," he teased gently.

"Of course." Her smile lit her eyes.

He felt his heart tug. There was something special about Gillian. He could deny it all he wanted, but it was there. And soon he'd have to make a decision what to do about it.

"Good night, Gillian," he said.

He leaned closer and brushed his lips against hers.

She blinked in surprise and then smiled again. "Good night," she said.

Falling into temptation, he brought her into his arms and kissed her again, before searching her face once more and then leaving.

He drove home wondering about his feelings for Gillian. He was attracted to her—emotionally and spiritually. It had been a long time since he'd felt this way about anyone. Yet, what was there about Gillian not to love?

The thought surprised him. For a moment he scarcely breathed. He slowly got out of the car and looked toward heaven.

"Father, this is unexpected. And I'm not sure it's wise. Yet I trust You to have a plan. If this is it, let me fall right in with it. If not, give me the strength to resist. Bless Gillian, Lord. And help us all do Your will, Amen."

Joe felt closer to the Father when he was outdoors in the beauty of the earth the Lord had created. He walked near the bluffs, hearing the sea, seeing only the dark void where the water surged. The sound was soothing. The rhythm as steadfast as the love of God.

He needed more practice in trusting. Maybe this was the next step. Dare he believe love when he experienced it again?

He had loved Pamela. Mourned her death. Now, was he falling in love again? Was this a second chance, if he dare take it?

"Help me, please, Lord," he said as he turned and headed for the house.

Gillian drove her new car to town to pick up Jenny. The rental company was sending someone to pick up their vehicle once Joe's men repaired the brake line.

She had a million things to do. First, see about her things in Las Vegas. She needed to fly back to get what she wanted to move to Maine and sell the old car.

She needed to finalize how she wanted to fix up the new space for a studio.

There was still lots to do with the house, plans for every room. Maybe it would be wiser to wait until she knew exactly where she was going to live. She might have to fix up that apartment over the studio.

If her father prevailed, the house would be his. After his move last night, she doubted he'd sell it to her, even if she offered top dollar.

How sad that she'd longed to know her father for so long and now was finding out he wasn't worth it. She prayed for a renewed relationship between her and her father, that he would change. *Please let him turn from his wicked ways, Lord, and see that family is important. We only have each other. It would be so nice to have some kind of relationship.*

Gillian found the Robinsons' home with no difficulty. Of

course the two little girls taking turns riding a bike on the sidewalk in front of the house made it a no-brainer. She parked and watched for a moment. The girl with the red curls had to be Sally Anne. She graciously let Jenny have a turn on her bike. When Jenny saw Gillian, she smiled and waved, riding over to the car.

Gillian got out and went to greet her. "Having fun?"

"I am. Sally Anne's bike is great. I wish my daddy would buy me one like it. Watch, I can ride all the way to the corner and back," she said proudly, shoving off and wobbling a little as she pedaled to the corner and stopped, turning the bike, and heading back. The smile on her face warmed Gillian's heart.

"Wish my daddy could see me," she said as she stopped next to Gillian.

"Your daddy sent me to pick you up. I have a quick errand to run at the attorney's office. Since I'm a little early, you can ride a bit more and then go with me. How does that sound?"

"Fun. Sally Anne, this is Gillian," Jenny called. Her friend ran over and said hi.

"It's nice of you to let Jenny ride your bike."

"It's okay. She doesn't have one of her own. I ride mine all around town, but only on the sidewalk, and I never run into people."

Gillian nodded solemnly. "Good etiquette," she said, just as Sally Anne's mother came to the front porch.

Gillian smiled and moved around the bike to head up the short walkway.

"Hello, I'm Gillian Parker. I live next door to the

Kincaids, and Joe asked me to pick up Jenny."

"He called to let me know. I'm Sally Anne's mother, Kimberley. Glad to meet you. Do you have time for a cup of coffee or something?"

"I'd love a glass of water," Gillian said. "I'll watch the girls play, if that's okay. I'm going to be teaching the second-grade Sunday School at Trinity. I just heard from Pastor John today. Does Sally Anne attend?"

"Yes. I heard Sarah Jane was pregnant. I'm glad they found someone right away. Do you have children?"

"No, but I've taught Sunday School for the last seven years."

Once Kimberley brought them each a glass of cold water, they sat companionably together on the front porch and chatted while the girls took turns on the bike. Gillian was just about ready to leave when she heard Sally Anne yell.

"Watch out!" The little girl began running up the street.

Gillian and Kimberly jumped up at the same moment and ran to the sidewalk and instinctively headed after Sally Anne even before they saw the tumble of bike and little girl. Jenny was lying still, the bike partly on top of her.

"*Oh, Lord, please let her be all right,*" Gillian said as she ran as fast as she could.

Sally Anne reached Jenny first and was crying. "Are you hurt?" she kept asking.

"Here, let me move the bike," Gillian said. She and Kimberley lifted it off the little girl, who was starting to move.

Her left knee was scraped and bleeding and there was a scrape on her chin.

"What happened?" Kimberley asked as Gillian carefully assessed the damage.

Jenny began to cry as she sat up. "My head hurts," she said, reaching for Gillian.

She gathered the little girl close and hugged her. "Goodness, a fall like that I'm not surprised. Do you hurt anywhere else?"

She thought it a good sign the little girl seemed to be able to move around with no discomfort. She brushed back the hair from her forehead, studying the abraded skin. A knot was already rising.

"Maybe you need a bit more practice riding," she said gently.

"It wasn't me. It was that man. He threw a stick at the bike. And then he laughed when I fell."

Gillian looked around. She didn't see anyone besides the four of them, but she did see a long stick on the sidewalk.

"What man, honey?" she asked.

"He was tall and had a hat," Sally Anne said. "And he was trying to make her fall." She looked at her friend. "Don't cry, Jenny. Gillian will make you feel better."

Gillian smiled at the child's faith in her abilities.

"Come on back to the house and we'll wash the scrapes and make sure there isn't anything more serious," Kimberley said.

"I'll have to call Joe."

"Let's see what's what before that. No sense worrying him if she's just scraped up."

Gillian stood up and helped Jenny to her feet, then

scooped her up. She weighed more than expected, but Gillian didn't care. This precious child had been injured. She wanted to cuddle her until all traces of the accident were gone.

She dreaded Joe's reaction, however. He was so protective about his daughter.

Jenny hugged Gillian, her tears subsiding. "I guess Daddy won't never let me have a bike now. But that man was mean. And he smelled bad."

"He sure was. You don't know who he was?"

She shook her head. "He had a hat. It covered some of his face. He was hiding behind the bushes and jumped out and scared me. Then he laughed when I fell down. Did I hurt Sally Anne's bike?"

"No, it looks fine," Gillian said, surveying the bike as Kimberley walked it home. Sally Anne was subdued as well.

By the time Gillian and Kimberley had washed the scrapes and put on some antibiotic ointment, it was past time to meet with Julian. Gillian called him to tell him why she was late and they rescheduled.

"I'm taking you home right away," Gillian told Jenny when the bandages were in place. "Your father is going to have a fit."

"It's not such a big deal," Kimberley said. "Kids fall all the time."

"I hope Joe sees it that way," Gillian said.

When she reached the Kincaid driveway, she turned in slowly. Jenny had been quiet all the way home. Even the offer of an ice cream cone had not excited her. Gillian should have collected her the instant she arrived rather than visit with

Kimberley. She hoped Joe wouldn't blow a gasket.

She walked the little girl around to the back, knowing the Kincaids used that door the most. Zack was sitting on a bench, working on a car part. He glanced up and then did a double take when he saw Jenny.

"Whoa, what happened to you? I didn't know this household was so accident prone."

Jenny went to stand beside him, studying the auto part in his hand. "I fell off Sally Anne's bike. Some bad man scared me and threw a stick at me." She wrinkled her nose. "And he smelled bad."

Zack raised his eyebrows and looked at Gillian.

"Seems like what happened," she said. "Jenny was brave and hardly cried at all. We fixed her up at the Robinsons' and came right home. Is Joe around?"

Zack jerked his head toward the house.

"He's on the phone with the shop. Honestly, he needs to heal fast and get back to work. He's so antsy he's driving me nuts."

"This'll cheer him up," she said morosely.

"Hey, it's not your fault."

Joe came to the door. "Thought I heard voices." He started out and caught sight of Jenny.

"What happened?" He ran over to her in lightning speed.

"I fell off Sally Anne's bike," Jenny said.

"I told you not to go riding, didn't I?" he said. Kneeling down beside her, he looked closely at her forehead and her knees. "Are you all right?"

She nodded. "Gillian fixed me."

He looked at Gillian. "How did this happen?"

She began to tell him, but as soon as she said Jenny had been riding the bike, he rose. "Why didn't you stop her? You know I don't want her doing dangerous things."

"Whoa, bro. What's dangerous about riding a bike on Water Street?" Zack asked in surprise.

"I don't want her injured. Look at her! She could have been seriously hurt."

Zack shrugged. "So, Jenny, break any bones?"

She shook her head.

"Knock out a tooth?"

She shook her head.

"Get a black eye?"

She turned to look at Gillian, who shook her head.

Jenny looked back at Zack.

"How about a sprained ankle?"

She shook her head.

Zack gave his brother a look. "Your daddy did that and more. We used to ride our bikes from here to town and back. And your daddy was a daredevil. Remember the time you dared Jason Wilcox to a race to city hall and back? That was the time you got the black eye. Mama was fit to be tied. Or how about when you and I went rappelling down the cliff and you fell and broke your arm. Or—"

"That's enough. I have enough sense to make sure Jenny doesn't do those things," Joe said.

"She needs to," Zack said. "Kids need to explore, push boundaries, find out what they're good at. Look at you, all that happened, yet here you are, safe and sound except for some burns gotten while playing hero. Would you have been able to help Gillian out the night of the fire if you didn't have confidence in yourself because of all you accomplished growing up? Give the kid some room, Joe. I know it's got to be hard. But she has to grow up. You can't wrap her up in safety and never let her spread her wings. What's she going to do when you're gone?"

"I like riding Sally Ann's bike. And I didn't fall. That stick jammed the wheel and then the bike went over," Jenny said.

"What stick?"

"Jenny said a man jumped from behind a hedge and threw a stick, causing her to fall. I didn't see anyone by the time I reached her, but if he ran away, I wouldn't have. I did see a stick. Check with Kimberley. Sally Anne saw him as well. But neither child can give a very good description."

"A man or a teenager?" Joe asked.

"A man, Daddy. He was big and had a hat. He was mean."

"The hat made the biggest impression on the girls. Who would do such a thing?"

"Can't imagine. I'm calling Sheriff Tate."

Joe looked at Gillian and his face softened. She looked worried to death.

"Hey, it isn't your fault. You brought her back. That's what counts."

"I still feel badly it happened."

"Ever fall when you were a kid?"

She nodded.

He glanced at Zack and then back to Gillian. "Zack's right. We were wild when we were boys. And I lived to tell the tales."

Jenny giggled. "Tell me how you were wild, Daddy," she said with glee.

"Later. Gillian was going to make cookies today. Do you want to help her?"

Gillian's surprise almost made Joe smile. He was not going to hold a childish mishap against her. Hard as it was to admit, maybe he had been just a tad overprotective.

"Yay! Chocolate chip?" Jenny asked, her face beaming with happiness.

"Is there any other kind?" Gillian asked, smiling at the little girl, then at her father.

"Make plenty," Zack suggested.

"Come over after you talk to the sheriff, will you?" Gillian asked.

"Yes. He may want to speak to Jenny as well. Jenny, mind Gillian."

He watched as they returned to Gillian's car. Jenny had already forgotten her accident. She was excited to be going to make cookies.

He was growing to respect Gillian more and more. Her advice wasn't casually made. She'd dealt with children a lot teaching Sunday School for years.

Zack was right—they'd been wild when they were children. He remembered his mother arguing with his father about letting them get into so much mischief. She was afraid for them but went along with letting them explore the neighborhood, the town, the sea. He only now appreciated how hard that must have been for her.

He was guilty of keeping Jenny too close. Too sheltered. But he loved her so much he ached thinking of any hurt she might experience. Yet adversity also help form people's character as they grew.

"I place her in Your hands, Lord. Take care of my daughter and let her grow in all ways, especially in faith and love for You, Lord. Thank You for the gift of her," he prayed softly.

She was a gift from God. And he had better remember the Lord had all things in control. Jenny was in good hands.

Chapter Ten

Gillian slid the last batch of cookies out of the oven when Joe knocked on the back door.

"Come in," she called.

Jenny leaned over the table, carefully placing cooled cookies on a plate to free the rack for those coming out of the oven.

"Hi, Daddy. Want some cookies?"

He smiled. "I see you've already sampled them."

The tell-tale chocolate around her mouth gave her away. A large glass with very little milk remaining showed she'd been doing that for a while.

"They're really good. I think Gillian makes the bestest cookies."

"She does, does she?"

Jenny nodded emphatically. "Gillian uses lots and lots of chocolate chips."

"The secret revealed," Joe said as he pulled out a chair and sat across from his daughter. "You feeling okay, punkin'?"

"Yes." She watched as Gillian carefully took the cookies off the hot sheet and placed them on the rack.

"We need to take some to Uncle Zack," she reminded.

"We sure do, and some for your daddy, beyond what he might eat here."

Gillian had seen the sheriff's car arrive at the house and leave a short time later. She wanted to know what the sheriff had said, but she wasn't sure she should bring it up in front of Jenny.

"Why don't you fix a plateful and take 'em to Uncle Zack now?" Joe asked. "I'll wait here until you get back."

In less than five minutes, Jenny was off carefully carrying the cookies home. Joe sat at the table, a large plate of cookies in the center, enjoying the warm cookies.

"So what did the sheriff say?" Gillian asked once Jenny was out of hearing distance.

"He called Kimberley to talk to her before he came. He doesn't have anything to go on. Even a tall teenage boy might look like a man to the girls. There haven't been any other similar situations reported. Tate seems to think it's a kid playing a mean prank. Her fall might have scared him enough not to do it again."

"I still feel badly it happened at all—especially on my watch."

Joe was quiet for a moment, then looked at her. "You and Zack are right. I'm keeping her too sheltered. She needs to experiment with life to grow and be capable when she's older. I don't want anything to happen to her, but in the long run a few scrapes and bumps won't leave lasting hurt."

"You need to trust her to God's care. He watches out over all of us. Remember how Jesus loved to have the children come to Him? I think the Father has a special spot in His heart for children."

"It's hard sometimes. She almost died in the car crash that killed her mother. I was days at the hospital praying she'd recover."

"And she did."

He nodded. "It was like getting her as a gift a second time. I was so grateful. I vowed I'd keep her safe forever."

Gillian smiled. "Would that we always could wrap children up safely and have them know only joy. True joy awaits. In the meantime, your job as daddy is to equip her for the future—whatever it may hold. Your parents let you grow and be adventuresome and as a result, you're a competent successful adult. Jenny deserves the same chance."

Joe munched on a cookie for a minute.

"So, want to go with me to buy her a bike? Better to get a good solid one she can ride around the yard than have her keep sneaking rides with her friends who live in town. Too dangerous there."

"Until she learns the rules, then maybe she can ride in town," Gillian suggested.

He opened his mouth to protest, then snapped it shut with a frown. "This isn't easy."

She laughed. "Have another cookie and let me pamper you for your brave decision."

A glimmer of amusement touched his eyes. "I'd need some more milk to go with them," he said.

"Coming right up."

When they both had more milk and cookies before them, Joe said, "Thanks for helping with Jenny. It's hard to raise a child alone."

He took another bite.

"It's hard to admit Pamela was leaving me when she crashed. She wanted to live in New York, have fun before she grew too old to enjoy it. Sophie said that she felt if a young person didn't get that wanderlust out of his or her system early, that chance to feel like they were exploring life, that they'd take it sooner or later. In our case, it was when Jenny was about two. I think Pamela felt hemmed in. We couldn't just take off for Boston or Portland without getting someone to watch Jenny. Money was tighter then than now."

"I'm sorry."

"Yeah, it does take a toll when a man finds he's not enough for his wife."

"I'm sure it wasn't like that. She just wanted to have fun. If she took Jenny with her, so she must have been planning on taking care of her. That would have limited her ability to kick over the traces and do whatever she wanted."

"Maybe."

"Or, maybe she wanted you to join them. Maybe a vacation was all she had in mind. Did she say where she'd be?"

Joe looked at her for a long moment. "Her note said she was leaving for New York. And yes, she gave the name of the hotel she planned to stay at."

"Did she take all her things with her?"

"She packed one suitcase. Traveling light." He fell silent for a moment. "In thinking about it, she didn't take much else. No pictures or anything like that."

The thought that his wife had not been planning to leave

for good was a new idea. He'd been so sure she'd been fleeing the life they had that he had never considered it merely a drastic measure to get him away from work and to pay some attention to his family for a little while.

Money had been tight. He'd been trying so hard to make a go of a risky venture that he poured his energy into getting cars turned around faster than promised. He wanted to build a solid reputation for dependability and excellent work.

And Pamela had paid part of that price. Home alone for hours with Jenny and no adults to talk to, except an octogenarian next door. Had she resorted to drastic measures to get his attention—and some time away from Rocky Point?

Had it only been for a vacation?

"It may be you'll never know for certain, but it sure gives you a better alternative to give to Jenny when she's older," Gillian said. "I know kids want to love their parents. Even now, after all these years of neglect and the hard words between us, I wish my dad wanted to be my dad."

"Some people shouldn't have children," Joe said.

"True. But I'm grateful to be here, so maybe what my dad's done in the past hasn't been all bad."

"I'd say he did one thing right," Joe said. "One of the hardest things to deal with for me is knowing exactly what to do to give Jenny the best life possible."

"She's lucky to have a dad who loves her so much. Let her try things. I bet she'll always have good memories of her childhood in Rocky Point."

"Unlike Zack," Joe said.

"I don't know. He sounded like he was having fun

remembering all the scrapes you got into as children. Maybe he needed his time away and now is ready to settle down."

"Or maybe he's a wanderer, never satisfied with life, always looking for more."

"Maybe. God has a plan for each of us, you know. And His plans may not be clear to us or what we want for others. But in His time, all is made clear. Your plan won't be the same as Zack's. Doesn't mean his is wrong."

"I wish he'd stick around," Joe said. He flexed his left hand.

"Itching?" Gillian asked sympathetically.

"A bit. Doc said to exercise both without doing any damage. But some flexibility is needed to keep the skin supple. I'm almost ready to go without bandages for this hand. The right one is still healing."

"Don't push it."

"We've got cars to renovate. I can't be sidelined for long."

"Ask Zack for help," she suggested.

Joe looked at her in surprise. After a moment he nodded.

"I should. He knows as much about the insides as I do— or he did. We used to break down and rebuild old cars when we were teens."

"Tell him you'd like him to stay," she suggested.

Joe shook his head. "Don't know if I want to get that gushy."

Gillian laughed.

"I like it when you do that," he said slowly.

She blinked and looked at him. "Do what?"

"Laugh."

Gillian immediately became self-conscious.

"Will you go out to dinner with me? Just the two of us. I promise not to strand you like your father did. I'd like to take you to one of the seafood places up the coast. I think you'd love it. It's right on the water and the catch is always fresh."

"I would love to. When?"

"Tomorrow night? I'll get Zack to babysit."

"Thank you. I'd like that."

"So tomorrow's the big day, right?"

"What?"

"Your first day of Sunday School at Trinity."

"Yes. I got the lesson plan from the pastor and have been preparing. I'm looking forward to it."

"Jenny will be so pleased when she finds out you're her new teacher."

The phone rang, and Joe rose and headed for the door. "I'm leaving. Have to get home."

Gillian nodded, waiting until he left to talk to Josie, one of her friends from Vegas. She was glad to hear from her, but she wished her time with Joe hadn't been cut short. Still, she had tomorrow night to look forward to.

Joe walked along the cliff, anticipation building as he thought about dinner tomorrow night. When he reached the house, Zack was back to cleaning a carburetor.

"I could use some help at the shop," Joe said. "Until my hands completely heal. You sticking around that long?"

Zack nodded.

"What about racing?"

"The car blew its engine last time out. The men are repairing it. I'm too far behind the leaders now to win serious money this year. Good time to take a break."

Joe didn't want to get mushy, but he felt a wave of feeling sweep through for his brother. They'd been close as kids. He'd like for them to be close again.

"I appreciate your coming home to help out. I've missed you."

That surprised Zack. He looked at Joe. "I've missed you, too. I wish you'd come watch me race sometime."

"I might do that."

He was hearing Gillian's words that God's plan for Zack wouldn't be the same as His plan for Joe.

Time to stop rebelling and accept.

Zack looked surprised again. Joe almost laughed. "Come to church with us tomorrow," Joe said.

"I don't know that I'm much of a church-going man anymore," Zack said.

"Then come for Jenny's sake. We'll give thanks for God's watching over you and keeping you safe all these years racing."

For a moment Joe thought Zack would agree. But as if the past reared up, he shook his head.

"I think it best if I keep visits to town to a minimum. I'll drive you down, if you like."

"We'll catch a ride with Gillian," Joe said.

He bet she wouldn't mind taking him and Jenny to church in the morning. Maybe they could all have lunch at Marcie's. Then tomorrow night it would be just he and Gillian.

Joe started for the house.

"I'll go by the shop on Monday, see if there is anything I can do," Zack said.

"I appreciate it."

Joe had no illusions that his brother would one day return to Rocky Point and go into business with him. They'd talked about doing something like that when younger, but the lure of the raceway drew Zack. Joe could see how life in Rocky Point would pale in comparison to the Grand Prix circuit.

Stepping inside, he wondered how long before his hands healed and his brother would take off for Europe again. Maybe he should make an effort to see Zack race. Jenny would love something like that.

"Hi, Daddy," Jenny said, sitting at the table, coloring in one of her animal coloring books.

"Hey, honey, how would you like to pick out a bike?"

Chapter Eleven

Gillian was pleased with the turnout at her Sunday School class. She had been told by Pastor John that the class often had more than twenty children.

There were fifteen well-behaved children that Sunday who had very positive attitudes. Soon she had all the children answering questions on the lesson. When it came time to color the picture relating to the lesson, she enjoyed hearing the chatter that went on as the children diligently colored the robes and background of the scene.

Jenny had proudly claimed friendship with the new teacher, and her friends Sally Anne and Melissa had chimed in, too.

The time flew by and soon class was over. She gave each child a hug and promised to be there next Sunday. Jenny waited until the end and then held Gillian's hand as they walked to the sanctuary.

"You're a good teacher," Jenny said.

"I'm glad you think so. There are lots of nice boys and girls in the class."

"I go to school with them, too."

Rocky Point was too small to have more than one

elementary school. So this Sunday School class was unlike her class in Las Vegas, where she had children from three different elementary schools.

Joe stood near the double doors leading into the sanctuary when they came through the garden from the Sunday School rooms to the front of the church.

"Daddy."

Jenny relinquished her grip on Gillian's hand to dance ahead to her father. He smiled and then lifted his gaze to Gillian.

"How did it go?" he asked, taken again with how pretty Gillian was. Could he trust what he longed to believe, that she would remain in Rocky Point? That she might even harbor some feelings for him?

"Very well. The children were fun and well behaved."

"Probably threatened by parents if they didn't behave on your first day. No one wants to scare you away."

She laughed. He loved the sound and the way her eyes lit up as if there were a bright light behind them.

"Zack didn't come?" she asked, looking around.

"Not today."

"Too bad. Don't you think he has to face her sometime?"

"Not if he can help it. Ready to go in?"

Gillian looked startled for a moment, then that smile came again.

"I am."

Joe felt some of the stares as he escorted Gillian and Jenny to the midpoint of the church and gestured for them to enter the row he normally sat in. He greeted those church members sitting close by and then sat beside Gillian. Jenny sat on the far side and was already reaching for her hymnal. It was the first time he'd come to church with another woman since Pamela died. He knew there would be speculation. He could deal with it. Could Gillian?

"After church, would you like to go to the café for lunch? Marcie doesn't work on Sunday but keeps the café open for the after-church crowd."

"I'd love to," she said.

Joe had no trouble giving thanks to the Lord when the quiet prayer time came. He was grateful for Zack's being home. Maybe they could mend some hurt there. He was grateful for Jenny's safety in the bicycle accident.

And more and more he was growing grateful that Gillian had moved in next door. He offered a prayer that her troubles would be small and that the house would be awarded to her and not her father.

Joe was surprised by Gillian's beautiful voice when they sang hymns. Although, hadn't she said she had been in her church choir in Nevada? She should join theirs. Except then she couldn't sit beside him during the service.

Pastor John's message was on a passage from the Sermon on the Mount. As he spoke of both daily lives and false prophets, Joe began to remember more and more about his last months with Pamela. He'd known her all his life.

She wouldn't have left him and taken their child. He'd been blind to other possibilities, yet the more he thought about his wife, the more he knew her running away had been at odds with her character.

Had he misjudged her?

As he had with Gillian at first. He'd seen what he expected to see rather than what was there. She had never once done or said anything to give him reason to suspect that she was a flighty, flashy, self-centered person. She'd been kind and generous. And up front about wishing to stay in Rocky Point and make a life for herself.

He glanced at her. She was focused on the pastor and didn't seem aware of anyone else. She had a genuine love for the Lord, which would prove an example to the children in her new Sunday School class and to others.

Quietly he asked the Lord's forgiveness and vowed to be open to whatever the Lord had in store for him.

When Joe and Gillian and Jenny entered the café after church, the first person Gillian saw was her father. Instantly on the alert, she nudged Joe and nodded toward Robert Parker, who was eating alone at a table.

"I hope he's not planning to make a scene."

"I'd like to go give him a piece of my mind about the other evening," Joe said in a low voice.

"No." Gillian caught his arm. "Let's not spoil our time together. He is who he is."

The hostess led them in the opposite direction, and Gillian was relieved.

Midway through their lunch, Robert came to the table. "May I?" he asked, pulling out the fourth chair.

Jenny looked at him, then at her father and Gillian. She didn't say anything.

Gillian took a breath. She so longed to be a cherished

daughter of loving parents, out for a Sunday dinner together.

"You have some nerve," Joe said, placing his fork on his plate. "Was that your strategy, make her vulnerable so she'd acquiesce to your demands? The attorney who wrote that will you claim was Sophie's will be back this week. We'll find out once and for all if Sophie signed it."

"Oh, that part's not a problem," Robert said airily. "I came to apologize for the other night. Sometimes my temper gets the best of me. Obviously she has fine friends who came to her rescue."

"You ought to grovel on the floor for such a stunt," Joe said. "What do you want now?"

"To tell Gillian my offer still stands. You can buy the place from me and live in the family homestead all your life if that's what you want. And from what I hear, it is."

"Maybe," she said.

Joe looked at her in surprise. Was she changing her mind?

Robert looked equally surprised. "Isn't that what you want?"

"Oh, I'll stay in Rocky Point. But whether in my great-grandmother's house or not depends on a lot of things. I'm renting a studio that has an apartment over it. Maybe I should move out of the house and rent that apartment. Much more convenient to my work, wouldn't you think?"

Robert glanced at Joe, then looked back at Gillian. "You're just like Sophie—the sentimental type. The house has been in the family for years. Surely you want that connection."

Gillian nodded. "It would be nice. But just being in Rocky Point, becoming part of the community, is enough. It's not as if those first Parkers that came lived in that house. It's the community that's important."

Joe hid a smile at the look of chagrin on Robert's face. Gillian was a perfect match for her father.

Robert's anger flared at Joe's smile. He rose. "You'll be sorry," he said and quickly left.

"Why did he get so mad?" Jenny asked.

"He's a grumpy old man. Let's not allow him to spoil our lunch," Gillian answered.

"He only wants the money," Joe said.

"I have faith in God's plan. I'm not going to worry about this anymore. If I inherit, I'll be grateful. If not, I'm still grateful it brought me here."

"I'm grateful for that, as well," Joe said.

He wasn't sure how far this relationship might go, but for the first time since Pamela's death, he was open to the possibility of forging bonds that would last a lifetime.

Gillian opened the door that evening shortly before six. Joe looked handsome in his dark suit, pristine white shirt and blue tie. He'd looked good at church, but now they were going to dinner, just the two of them. Her heart rate kicked up a notch as she smiled.

"Ready to go?" he asked, taking in the dress she wore, a pretty, casual summer dress in maroon with white trim.

"You look beautiful," he said.

"This is a special treat." She went for her purse and light jacket. "Ready."

The drive up the coast was lovely, with flowers starting to show in some gardens and trees leafing out. They saw the sea intermittently as the road curved around obstacles and up and down hills. Reaching Porterville well before the seven o'clock reservation, they took a few moments to walk around the old whaling town.

Gillian was fascinated with the historic buildings, some of which had plaques in front describing who'd lived there in the 1800s.

"Wow, what history," she exclaimed at the top of one slight hill, with a direct view to the sea. "Rocky Point wasn't a whaling town, was it?"

"No, general fishing. The wives and widows of the whalers banded together here and ran things pretty well. There were enough men around to give a sense of stability and protection. But when the whalers were gone, it was a predominantly female society. The local historical society has a lot of information on daily life from diaries that were donated. We do, too, in Rocky Point."

Gillian took his arm as they strolled back through the town on the way to the restaurant. She was having a wonderful time with Joe, and was able to put all her concerns aside and concentrate on enjoying the evening.

Dinner was delicious—fresh halibut with vegetables and a delicious chocolate mousse for dessert. They sipped coffee and talked well into the evening, ending only when Joe said they should be leaving because of the long drive back.

"Tell me some of Rocky Point's history," she said as they headed toward their own town.

Joe complied, making the tales of the fishermen and their families carving a settlement on the rocky coast of Maine both exciting and inspiring. He threw in some tales from men who served in the Revolutionary War, who marched with Sherman in the Civil War and even one or two who had served at Omaha Beach.

"What about your family or mine?" she asked.

"As I recall, Sophie's grandfather served in the Civil War, and her father in the Great War. Same as my grandfather. There have been Kincaids in most of the skirmishes from the beginning. And Tuckers, which was Sophie's maiden name. Some Parkers, too. Have Margaret at the historical society help you look up more."

"Maybe I'll look into it," Gillian said. "Imagine having a family that can be traced back generations."

"I don't have to imagine. I live it."

"And Jenny. She's so lucky to have such a stable family life. You're a wonderful father."

"She misses having a mother."

Gillian became silent, remembering her own mother and how much she missed her. How much worse would it have been to have never known her.

Joe pulled into the space beside her house and switched off the engine.

"Thank you for a wonderful time and a delicious dinner."

"The pleasure was all mine."

He walked her to the front door. The porch light had been left on and there was a light showing from inside.

"You thought ahead, I see," he said.

"I don't like coming home to a dark house."

"But here I feel like I'm in a spotlight," he said, standing beneath the full glare of the porch light.

She grinned. "And that's bad because...?"

"Because I want to kiss you good night and not have anyone driving by see," he said slowly, reaching out with his left hand and drawing her to the far end of the porch where the light wasn't as bright.

Moving slowly, as if giving Gillian every chance to stop if she wished, he drew her into his arms and kissed her.

She kissed him back, happiness blossoming within.

When several seconds had passed, he gently pulled back. "Thank you for coming with me. I enjoyed every moment."

"Me, too."

He kissed her again and then led her to the front door.

"Go inside. I'll wait to hear you lock up."

She nodded, feeling dazed and as if she were walking on clouds. "Good night," she said. In only seconds the door shut behind her and she locked up, feeling cherished and secure because he'd waited.

Joe hummed a favorite song as he drove the short distance home. The evening had been perfect. He was pleased Gillian seemed to have enjoyed it as much as he had. And if she was a curious as she appeared about the history of Rocky Point and her family, it gave them another avenue of commonality. He loved the history of this area of Maine. Would that give them another bond?

Gillian made her best effort planning dinner the next morning. She wanted to wow the Kincaids, especially one particular one. She'd slow-cooked a pot roast in the afternoon. Whipping up a pecan pie for dessert that morning, she enjoyed herself as she moved around the kitchen. Humming quietly, she thought about the evening before and how much she'd enjoyed herself.

Caroline Everett called mid-morning shortly after Gillian had removed the pie from the oven.

"How are you settling in, my dear?" Caroline asked.

"Fine. How are you? How is Maud doing?"

"That's why I called. She's coming home today. Her doctor said if she takes it easy and uses a walker, she can return home. She's so impatient to leave, I think she drove the nurses crazy. I'm calling to see if you wanted to ride with me to get her. She's dying to see you again."

"I'd love to. What time would you leave?"

"Right after noon. I want to be there around one."

"I'll be ready."

Maud was delighted to see them when they arrived. In no time, Gillian had her suitcases in the trunk while Caroline walked slowly beside her friend and then helped fold the walker when Maud was seated in the front seat. Gillian had insisted she'd have more room there.

The drive back was fun. Gillian could imagine her great-grandmother in the midst of this gathering, and from what the others said, she was getting a good picture of the woman she'd never meet.

"Do you want to come in and see what I've done to the house so far?" she asked when they reached home. "Can you manage the three porch steps?" she asked Maud, suddenly wondering if it had been a wise invitation.

"I'm up to it. Show us what you've done."

After a brief tour of the downstairs, Caroline went upstairs with Gillian while Maud went to sit in Sophie's favorite chair on the ground floor.

A few minutes later, when they joined her in the front room, she held an old photo album in her hands. "Want to know something about your folks?" she asked.

"Yes." Gillian dragged a chair up next to hers. Caroline smiled and sat on the sofa.

Opening the old-fashioned book, Maud looked at the first picture.

"Wow, this takes me back. This is Sophie's only child, Jonathan. That's Sophie and your great-grandfather, Jarred. Didn't they make a handsome couple?" She studied the old picture, while Gillian leaned closer.

She'd seen these photos and wondered who everyone was. A young woman with waves in the style of the twenties stood proudly next to a handsome man.

"Jarred died too young. Before their grandson was born. Such a shame. Sophie grieved his passing for a long time." Maud glanced at Caroline. "You remember."

Her friend nodded.

Looking back at the book, she turned a page. "I haven't seen these pictures in ages."

Slowly they leafed through the album, Maud identifying people as she went along. Gillian studied each one avidly, soaking up the knowledge. She'd write the names beside them after Maud left.

The second album had photographs of Robert as a baby, with his father and mother. Then as he grew older, with just his mother. She did not look happy in later pictures.

"Sophie mourned her son, and never got close to his widow, or Robert. The widow, what was her name?"

"Eliza, I think," Caroline said.

"She complained that Sophie should have made things easier for them. But Sophie didn't have a lot of money. And she objected to that woman's lifestyle."

Gillian wondered if her father's childhood had dictated the direction he had taken as an adult—always trying to get rich quick, no matter who might suffer along the way.

"Here's your father at the beach at the base of the bluffs," Maud said, studying one photograph. "He came most summers, if only for a week or two for a few years after Jonathan died. Once he spent the entire summer."

There was a photograph of a much younger Robert beside Sophie, and both were smiling. Gillian wished they could have continued to share whatever happiness brought smiles to their faces in that picture.

When the album ended, Maud sighed. "Brings back lots of good memories."

"You need to get home," Caroline said. "Gillian, let us know when you need help here. Even if I can't do much, I have a healthy grandson who can wield a mean paintbrush."

Gillian smiled. "I'll be sure to let you know. The more help I have, the quicker things will get done."

After the ladies left, Gillian checked dinner, cooked the side dishes and packed everything in a tote to bring to Joe's.

When she knocked on his back door, Joe let her in. In a surprising move, he hugged her, then kissed her forehead.

"Hi," she said breathlessly.

"Welcome. Something smells great," he said. Walking past, she drew in a deep breath to calm rioting nerves.

"Good. I hope it tastes that way. How's Jenny?"

"Except for the scabs on the scrapes, she's as good as new. She and her uncle are playing race cars on some video game."

She'd begun to withdraw items from the tote and placed the Crock-Pot on the counter. Taking out the other food, she paused in her search for serving plates and noticed his hand. "Joe, your left hand doesn't have a bandage."

He raised his hand and slowly flexed it. The skin on his palm looked pink. "Went back to the doctor's this morning. It's not quite as good as new, but almost. I have cream to use and strict instructions not to overdo things."

"And your right hand?"

"Getting better."

"I bet you have mixed feelings about that," she said.

"How so?"

"Once you're back to normal, Zack will leave."

"True. But he's agreed to help in the shop for a while. He's been great with Jenny. My hope now is that he won't be gone so long before coming home again."

She tilted her head slightly. "You're different," she said.

He nodded. "Happier, I think. Because of you and what you said about Pamela. And about trusting in the Lord and His plan for my life. I'm open to whatever path He puts before me." He walked closer. "Can I help with dinner?"

"It's all ready. Once I dish it up, we can eat." She peered around him. The table had already been set. "You can call the others in."

The conversation around the dinner table was fun and lively. From time to time Gillian would pause, look around and give thanks for her wonderful neighbors and that they included her in their family.

When Joe mentioned the painting needed at the studio, Gillian chimed in with the colors she'd chose and the plans she had for the place.

"Don't forget you promised to go bicycle shopping with us," Joe said.

After dinner they moved to the living room, where Zack and Jenny resumed their video game. Joe and Gillian sat on the sofa and talked more about her plans.

As it grew dark, Gillian rose and headed to the kitchen. "I'm going to clean up."

"I'll help," Joe said.

Zack gave them a knowing look and said he was too caught up in the game to leave.

Gillian laughed and smiled at Joe. "No helping. You take care of your hands. You can keep me company if you like, though."

"I can handle that."

As she began rinsing the dishes, she glanced at him. "What do you think of my chances for the house? I really want to decorate it. Not all at once. That I can't afford."

"I think the letter Sophie wrote shows her true intentions.

She wanted you to have it."

"I think so, too. And I plan to do all I can to get it."

"The Kincaids are ready to help in any way we can."

"I'm counting on you," she said with a bright smile.

Her heart blossomed with the intensity of her feelings for Joe. He proved he was on her side. Together they could face anything!

When the dishes were finished, Gillian was reluctant for the evening to end. But it was growing late, already dark outside.

"Want to take a short walk?" he asked, as if loathed to end their time together.

"Sure." Ignoring the fact her car was in the driveway, she'd relish the walk.

"I have a jacket you can wear. It'll be a little cool."

When he draped his windbreaker around her shoulders, Gillian snuggled into it, smelling his manly scent in the jacket. She zipped it up and laughed. It was way too large for her, but the wrists were elastic and kept the sleeves from falling over her hands.

It was dark, but there was enough light from the stars to see where to walk along the bluff. Joe didn't let them go too near the edge, only close enough to hear the surf.

"I can't wait to go swimming in the sea. When does it get warm enough?" she asked.

"Never, not that freezing-cold water ever stopped us as kids, or Jenny. On a really hot day, the cold water feels good. But it never gets really warm, not like southern beaches. The cove is wide and we often take picnics there in the summer.

Jenny loves to play in the moist sand, and we do venture forth for short swims."

"Even if I'm renting that apartment in Rocky Point, I can come here once in a while, can't I?" Gillian asked.

"You can come as often as you want. The beach isn't private, just difficult to get to, so it's not used much except by my family. Sophie used it when she was younger, but the last twenty years or so she felt it was too much effort to climb back up. She'd like knowing you were enjoying it. I'd like knowing you were enjoying it—preferably with me."

She tried to see him in the darkness, but could only see his silhouette against the starry sky. "Me, too," she replied, wondering if he meant what she thought he said, or was it his way of being polite?

"So we'll plan picnics on the beach."

"Yes."

And more? She hoped so.

He reached out and took her hand. Gillian's heart began racing. She loved the feeling of his larger hand holding hers. She felt safe and secure, and once again cherished. Was Joe feeling what she was feeling? She dare not ask—in case the answer was no. But she suspected the love she already felt was growing and prayed he was falling in love with her, too.

Chapter Twelve

Gillian put in a full morning's work at the new studio. The place was not in bad shape, but it obviously had been empty for a while as the dust was thick everywhere. She swept, dusted and carted everything to the large dumpster in the rear of the building.

Joe's shop was buzzing. She propped the door open to get the studio aired out and could hear the noise from the shop. The men talked amicably, but too quietly for her to hear. A radio blared music and the sound of the renovations were erratic but constant.

She stopped before noon to get washed up before heading to the café.

When she entered, Marcie spotted her immediately and came to greet her. "Here for lunch?" she asked.

"I am. I've been working all morning at the studio and don't want to take time to go home. There's tons more to be done."

Marcie led her to a table and then sat down with her. "So what do you recommend?" Gillian asked.

"The sisters have a fabulous crab salad special today. That's what I'm having. I'll join you, if I may."

"Sounds good. I'll have the special, too."

A waitress delivered two glasses of iced water and took their orders.

"How are things going?" Marcie asked.

"Great. I'm starting in on fixing up the studio. Joe offered the services of his brother for any modifications I want. He would do it himself, I'm sure, if his hands hadn't been burned. Did you know the left hand is free of bandages now?"

"Sounds like he's healing fast. How much longer on the right?"

"He's not sure, but if sheer willpower alone would bring it about, he'd be healed now."

"God will heal it in His time."

"The burns have given Joe a chance to spend time with Zack," Gillian said, watching her friend carefully. "You okay with that?"

Marcie laughed. "I feel like everyone in town is walking on eggshells around me. He dumped me—at the altar, granted—but it was ten years ago. I'm fine. I wish he had handled things differently, but he didn't. I moved on." She glanced around the café proudly. "I've made a good life for myself here."

"I hope I can as well," Gillian said.

"And I hope Joe finds someone he can fall in love with again." Marcie looked at Gillian. "I think he's falling for you. And you sure light up when he's around."

Gillian dropped her gaze to her water glass, unsure how to proceed. "I admit I find him fascinating. But I'm not sure we know each other well enough yet."

"But you could be falling for him."

Gillian smiled and met her friend's eyes. "Yes, definitely. And for Jenny, too."

Their salads arrived, and the food was delicious. Gillian knew Marcie took care to make sure she offered the best at a low price. The restaurant was filling up and almost everyone who passed had something to say to Marcie. Several spoke to Gillian, and she greeted everyone in turn. She was accepted and was beginning to fit in.

When Marcie mentioned her new aerobics studio and groups starting soon, several women expressed interest. Gillian took their names and phone numbers and promised an announcement in the newspaper to let everyone know in plenty of time to sign up.

"A very productive lunch," she said when she and Marcie had finished eating. "Networking at its very best."

"We call it being neighborly. I want to sign up, too. You'd think I'd get plenty of exercise here, but lately I'm doing more office work and less work on the floor. I think a bit of aerobics would do wonders."

"Exercise is very beneficial. Even into old age. I have a program for older folks, using chairs and sitting for a good part of the time. More stretching and movement than aerobics. So it's something we can all do throughout our lives."

"Sounds like fun. Sign me up."

Gillian agreed. She enjoyed Marcie and knew they would become great friends as time went on.

As she walked back to the studio after lunch, she saw Joe's

car parked outside the car shop. And a man doing something to a tire.

"Hey, what are you doing?" she yelled, running toward him.

He stood suddenly, glanced at her and then took off running in the opposite direction. He wore faded jeans, a windbreaker and a ball cap pulled low. She couldn't get a good look at him, but she knew he was up to no good the way he ran.

Her shouts brought Zack, Joe and Frank running from the shop.

"What happened?" Joe asked when he saw Gillian.

"Some man was fiddling with your tire."

The one in question was flat, a large slice in the side.

"Whoa. He did a job on it," Zack said, stooping down to examine the puncture closely.

"Who'd do that?" Frank asked.

"I'll get the sheriff over to see if he can find out," Joe said, turning back to the shop to use the phone.

Zack glanced around. "What did he look like?" he asked.

"Like most men around here. Tall, dressed in jeans and a jacket with a ball cap on his head. He matched the description of the guy who caused Jenny to crash."

"Nothing else?"

She shook her head, drew in a deep breath. "Wait. Do you smell that?" She took in another breath, then shook her head. "For a moment I thought I smelled liquor. Too long in Vegas, I guess."

"It's faint, but I smell it, too," Frank said. He walked away from the car in the direction the other man had run. "Might mean something, might just be something carried on the breeze."

Joe came back out of the shop and walked up beside Gillian. "Tate will be here soon. And there haven't been any other reports of malicious mischief. For some reason he's targeting you and me."

Zack leaned against the car and gazed off down the street. "So what have you two done to make someone angry?"

"Taken the house from my father," Gillian said.

"Nothing," Joe said at the same time.

"It wasn't my father cutting the tire, however," Gillian said. "And I don't see him as someone who would cause a child to fall."

"If the fire had been at our house instead of yours," Zack said, "I'd say Joe was the target."

"It was Gillian's car that was damaged."

"On the way home from driving you to town. Maybe someone thought you'd be in the car on the way home, too."

Joe stared at his brother and then glanced at Frank. The other man had a speculative look on his face.

"Ben Ostler," Joe said.

"Who?" Gillian asked.

"Someone you've probably never met. He worked for me until a few weeks ago when I had to let him go. He has a bad drinking problem."

The sheriff's car pulled up behind Joe's and Sheriff Tate Johnston got out. He joined the small group at the rear of Joe's car, studying the tire for a moment.

"Try Ben Ostler," Joe said quietly. "Jenny said the man who threw the stick smelled bad, and Ben has a real drinking problem—that's the reason I fired him. He's got a grudge, I'm sure."

"Strong accusations, Joe," Tate said. "We've all known Ben forever."

"Drink makes men do things they wouldn't ordinarily," Zack offered.

"I'll check it out. Anyone see anything?"

"I did. I came from the café and saw a man kneeling by the tire. I didn't recognize him, so I called out. He stood and ran that way," Gillian said, pointing down the street.

"Description?" Tate asked.

She gave what she had, telling him it could be the same man that Jenny saw, from the description. No one got a good look at his face due to the hat pulled low.

"I'll look into it now," Tate said

"If it's Ben, he has to be stopped," Zack said.

"Yes. If we can prove he did any of it. Why Gillian's house, though?"

"Don't have a clue," Zack said.

Gillian shook her head. "I don't even know the man. Did he have a grudge against Sophie and took it out on me?"

"Doubt it. Everyone loved Sophie. Plus I can't ever think of a time Ben would have had any dealings with her," Joe said.

Tate promised to call them if he turned up anything.

After he left, Joe smiled at Gillian. "Working on your studio, I see."

"I am. Maybe you and Zack can come with me now and

see what I want done before opening."

He nodded. "Frank, I'll be back to check on that manifold in a few minutes," Joe said.

Gillian pointed out the improvements to the space she wanted—a large mirror on one wall, more dressing rooms in the back, also with mirrors. The office space needed shelves, and she wanted a surround-sound system for the music to exercise by. The floors, while of hardwood, needed sanding and refinishing.

There was a lot to do, and she held her breath while Zack and Joe discussed how long the work would take and who could do what.

Joe wanted to do more himself, but Zack and Gillian both protested.

"You'll be heading back to the race circuit before this will be finished," Joe said to his brother.

"No, I'll stay and see it through. Like I said, I'm pretty much out of the running this year."

"That's great, thank you. Once you two decide how long it will take, I can begin advertising for the classes and hopefully signing up some clients," Gillian said.

"I'll get a tape measure and get some measurements and be able to get some of the lumber today," Zack said. He nodded and headed out to the shop.

"Did you hear anything from Julian today?" Joe asked as he and Gillian were left alone in the studio.

"No. I was busy all morning, and didn't have a chance to call. I don't know if that's good news or not."

Joe stepped closer, brushing her cheek with his fingertips.

"You have a smudge there."

"Oh, no, I went to lunch in town like this."

He laughed. "I'm sure no one minded. We are all working at something. Call Julian. Maybe the news is good."

Gillian was afraid to find out. Yet delaying things wouldn't change the outcome. She nodded and pulled out her cell phone to call the attorney. His secretary answered.

"It's Gillian Parker. I wondered if Julian had heard anything from the Boston lawyer," she asked, her gaze fixed on Joe.

His calm demeanor helped her keep her cool, even though her heart raced. Would the house be hers? If not, she had the comfort that at one time at least, Sophie had wanted her to have it.

"Julian had an unexpected court appearance this morning," the secretary said. "He'll be in touch with the man as soon as he gets back."

"Thanks," Gillian said. She ended the call and shook her head at Joe.

"No news yet. Now I'm disappointed. I wish the suspense would just end so I'd know one way or the other. I have such plans for the house. But if I have to leave, I'm not putting my heart into renovations."

"The offer stands for the apartment upstairs," Joe said.

"I know. I appreciate that. Maybe it would be even better to be over the studio. No problem commuting in bad weather."

"I doubt if the weather is bad enough to keep you away from town that many clients will come, either."

"Good point."

"It would be better for you to be at Sophie's house," he said. "I'd want you there. Closer."

Gillian nodded, her heart rate speeding up just a little. She wanted to be closer, too.

Joe had scarcely left when her cell rang.

"Gillian, it's your father," Robert said. "I'd like to see you, now if that's convenient."

"I'm in town," she said.

"Perfect. I'm at the Rocky Point Inn. Maybe you could swing by."

Gillian looked at her dusty jeans, remembered the smudge on her face. "It'll take me a few minutes to clean up. I could be there in about twenty," she said, already walking toward the restroom, hoping there were enough paper towels.

Now what did he want? she wondered as she splashed water on her face, making sure to get all the dirt on her face and arms. As she brushed her hair she thought about taking someone with her—like Joe. But he couldn't be with her all the time.

At least she couldn't get stranded today.

She still hoped for a relationship and maybe this was an opened door. "I hope so, Lord," she said, as she walked to her car. "Let us build some trust and affection, if it is Your Will."

The inn sparkled in the afternoon sunshine. The light breeze brought fragrances of the early flowers. She entered, wishing she'd taken time to go home to change.

The inn was away from the sea, set among soaring trees, some which would provide shade for the outside area during the summer.

Robert came to the lobby as soon as he'd been summoned by the front desk. He wore a suit, looking professional and businesslike. Gillian watched as he looked around for her, spotting her a second later and smiling genially as he crossed the large room to her.

"Come, let's get a drink on the veranda," he said as he escorted her to the side of the inn, where tables were spaced on the terrace.

"Lemonade, please," Gillian said when the waitress came for their order.

"Make it two," he added.

"I'm leaving Rocky Point," Robert said, coming instantly to the point.

"When?"

"This afternoon. I have business to attend to in California."

She sipped her lemonade and was surprised at a twinge of disappointment that filled her. Was this going to be the last time she saw him?

"Did you hear about the house?" she asked.

Was this the real reason? Had she prevailed?

"Either way it goes," he replied, "I never planned to stay. I want to sell. I'm still open to a bid from you, you know."

Gillian slowly shook her head. "I felt very special when I thought Sophie had left me the house. Like she was reaching out to me as a family member. But if she wanted you to have it, I still feel there was purpose in the first will—to draw me here to a special place where our family has had roots maybe even from before the Revolutionary War. I've never felt like I belonged anywhere before. I do here."

He nodded, his gaze fixed her face. "You'll fit in here. Something I never did."

"Where do you fit in?" she asked gently, still wishing to know more about him.

He met her eyes and smiled. "I'm a wandering kind of guy. There've been places I've enjoyed, but there's always more to see. I don't think I'd ever be happy in one town, one house."

"With one wife or one daughter," she said sadly.

He was silent for a moment.

"The call of the unknown, the adventure always waiting beyond the horizon proves stronger than wanting to stay anywhere. I thought of your mother over the years. And I admit to still being shocked that she's dead. She was younger than I am."

"Death can come unexpectedly," she said.

"True."

Gillian took a sip and then placed her glass back on the table.

"Either way the lawyers decide, I'm planning to stay in Rocky Point. If you inherit, I don't know if I'll buy or not. I can rent the apartment over the studio. Maybe I'm not meant for home ownership," Gillian said.

"Last chance to buy the house," Robert said with a wry grin.

He seemed uncertain, almost nervous, glancing around the courtyard, then back at Gillian.

"Then I'll pass."

His smile faded. Silence reigned for a moment. "Maybe I'll come back one day to see you."

Her smile was genuine. "I'd like that. Come whenever."

He studied her for a moment, then slowly nodded. "Maybe I will."

She reached out her hand and caught his, squeezing slightly. "We don't know each other very well, but you're my father. You'll forever be welcomed in my home, no matter what."

He studied their hands and slowly turned his hand over to squeeze hers back.

Gillian's cell rang, but she ignored it. The time with her father was too precious. She'd call back when she alone.

"Where in California are you heading?" she asked, releasing his hand and sitting back. Sipping the lemonade, she felt like a normal daughter spending time with her father. There were few memories between them—and not many of them good. But that didn't mean she couldn't make more as she had the chance.

"San Francisco. I've got an investment opportunity to explore."

He spent a few minutes going over the basics as Gillian simply sat and let him talk. She thought she'd caught a glimpse of the charming man her mother had loved.

"I'll need to be going," Robert said a short time later. He rose and Gillian jumped up, too, surprising them both by coming to hug him.

"Take care, Dad," she said.

He nodded and turned to reenter the inn. Pausing near

the door, he looked back. "I'll call you."

She nodded, doubting it, but she'd hope so, anyway.

Walking back to her car, she looked at her phone. Julian had called. She pressed redial and in only moments had the attorney on the line.

"Seems as if there are some irregularities with the Boston will," Julian said. "In discussing the situation with the other lawyer, we feel there needs to be more investigation into the situation. But neither of us believe Sophie was the signer. Looks as if the will I drew up will be the one probated."

"Where does that leave my father?" she asked, leaning against her car and looking at the inn. Was Robert's departure an indication he knew what was going on?

"Up for fraud charges, possibly. Or more likely, for Sophie's sake, we'll ignore the irregularity and move on. I'll be in touch when I know more."

"Thank you, Julian," she said. She got into her car and headed for home.

She wanted to tell Joe the news. And go with them to get Jenny's bike. She knew the little girl was going to be delighted.

Jenny waited in the yard when Gillian turned in. She waved and ran to the car once Gillian stopped.

"Are we going to get my bicycle soon?" she asked.

"Up to your father."

"He said it was up to you, when you had time."

"Let me clean up first. We have plenty of daylight left for you to ride if we get a good bike," Gillian said, giving the child a swift hug. "Want to come in and wait while I change?"

"Okay. Uncle Zack isn't going. Daddy said maybe you'd

like dinner at the café as a reward for going with us."

Gillian laughed, her heart blossoming with love for this child. "I do not need anything as a reward for going with you. Your happiness with your new bike will be reward enough. But I'd love to have dinner with you."

"I love you, Gillian," Jenny said, throwing her arms around Gillian's waist.

"I love you, too, Jenny." She hugged her back.

When they went into the house, Gillian said, "Tell me what color bike you want."

"Pink. It's my favorite color." The child talked about where she could ride and how good she'd be and now she could ride with her friends and not be the only girl in second grade who didn't have a bike. But she hadn't forgotten the horse, either, because she asked Gillian again if she was getting a horse.

Gillian laughed and wondered if she'd eventually end up owning a horse someday.

Gillian was ready to walk to Joe's house with Jenny for the great bicycle hunt when her phone rang.

"Gillian, Tate just called and said he has Ben Ostler in custody. I need you to come with me to see if he's the man you saw," Joe said.

"We were just heading your way. Be there in a minute."

"As soon as we are finished at the sheriff's, we can shop for that bicycle. Did Jenny ask you about dinner?"

"Yes, and I think that's a great idea."

"I'll pick you two up in a minute. We might need the truck if we find a bicycle."

A few moments later Gillian was in the front seat of the truck, Jenny safely seat belted in the backseat of the extended cab. As they drove down to Rocky Point, she couldn't help thinking they looked like an average American family—parents taking their daughter somewhere.

Looking at Joe she felt her heart swell with love for him. Just as it had earlier for Jenny. She knew he had issues with the painful end of his marriage. But she loved him and realized she'd like to build a life with him. Maybe have children together and raise them in love. He was a wonderful father. Jenny was happy, well adjusted and thriving. He'd be that good to any and all children he had.

She thought about the kisses they'd shared. That had to mean something, right?

Trust was an issue. She prayed that if God wanted Joe in her life, He would open both their eyes to that fact. And if not, to remove the yearning desire of her heart so she could move on and be open to another relationship.

She ended the prayer with asking that Joe love her as she did him. It might not be God's plan, but if it was, she wanted Him to know that was in her heart as well.

Then she told him about her father. And that she would be staying in Rocky Point with no further problems with her father.

Joe squeezed her hand when she finished, saying simply, "I'm glad."

The sheriff's office was not as large as Gillian had expected. A big open area with several desks facing each other, a counter behind which a dispatcher sat with a switchboard and swivel chair. There were about a dozen metal chairs in the waiting area. A hallway opened in the back.

"Hey, Joe. Tate's expecting you," the dispatcher said. "All of you, actually," she added with a smile for Jenny.

Joe knew the way.

Tate rose from his desk when they stepped into his office. "Have a seat. I'll take you back to see Ben in a moment. I wanted to review things with you first. Jenny, do you remember the man who made you fall?"

She nodded her head.

He looked at Gillian. "Do you think you could identify the man by the tire?"

"I'm not sure. He had on a hat and only glanced my way for a second. I can try."

"This is not the big city, but we do take law enforcement seriously here. I've asked a few men in for a makeshift identification lineup. I'll take you each separately, if that's okay?"

Jenny looked at her dad.

"Go with Tate," he said. "You're going to see several men. You tell Tate which one was the one who caused you to crash," Joe said.

The two of them left.

Joe looked at Gillian. "I can't believe it's Ben. He used to work for me. He's a good man—just has trouble controlling his drinking."

"It may not be him. Maybe it's a transient or someone," she said.

Tate and Jenny returned in a few minutes. She went to sit by her dad, her eyes on Gillian.

"She's not to talk until you leave the room," Tate explained to Gillian.

They went to a room that had a one-way mirror on the right side. There were five men, all dressed in jeans, jackets and ball caps. Gillian looked at each one, recognizing one she'd seen before at the café and another in church. The fourth in line was the man who had been by the tire.

Tate escorted her back.

"It's Ben. Both identified him," he said entering the office.

"Has he said anything?" Joe asked.

Tate shook his head.

"Retaliation," Joe said. "From being fired a few weeks ago."

"But why me?" Gillian asked.

Both men were silent while contemplating that question.

"No reason I know of," Tate said.

"Let's ask him. You have enough to arrest him, don't you?" Joe asked.

The sheriff nodded and went out of the room.

"Gillian, would you take Jenny outside while we speak with Ben?" Joe asked.

She wanted to hear what the man had to say, but she knew Joe didn't want his daughter there. She was glad to be of help.

"Sure. Maybe Jenny and I will walk down to the café and get a dish of ice cream. How does that sound?" she asked the little girl.

"Chocolate?" Jenny asked as she jumped up and ran to Gillian. "With sprinkles?"

"Works for me," Gillian said, taking her hand. She nodded to Joe and left.

Joe rose and paced to the window. He turned when Tate and Ben entered the room. The man in custody glared at Joe.

"You shouldn't have fired me, Kincaid. Where can I get work in town with that hanging over me?" His words were slightly slurred.

"How can you hold a job anywhere if you're drunk all the time? Especially a job that could get you or someone else hurt with inattention or clumsiness?" Joe countered as anger rose. "So you were after me—revenge for firing you?" he asked.

Ben glanced at the sheriff and then at Joe. "Don't know what you're talking about."

"I'm talking about scaring my daughter when she was riding a bike and causing her to fall. About slashing my tire. What about tampering with Gillian's car and causing it to crash?"

Ben glanced at the bandage still on Joe's right hand. Joe narrowed his eyes.

"Did you set the fire behind Gillian's house?"

Ben looked surprised. "It wasn't your house?" he said, then scowled.

Tate pushed him toward a chair. "Sit. We have some things to discuss."

Ben glared at Joe. "Shouldn't have fired me."

"You shouldn't have been drunk."

"A man needs a little libation to help him through the day."

Tate took charge. "Ben Ostler, you are under arrest for numerous offenses." He listed the charges, read him his rights and asked if he wanted an attorney present.

"I can't afford a lawyer," Ben whined. "Call my wife. Tell

her to find someone who will take credit."

Tate placed the call.

"Ellen said you're on your own," he relayed after speaking a few moments with Ben's wife.

The man seemed to deflate.

Joe almost felt sorry for him. Until he remembered how he'd put people he loved in danger.

The thought surprised him.

People he loved.

Not just his daughter. Gillian.

When he thought about her possibly being burned, or being seriously injured in the car crash, his throat closed up. He gave another brief prayer of thanksgiving to God for sparing her.

He stood. "If you don't need me anymore, I have to go." He wanted to make sure Gillian and Jenny were safe. And then he had to tell them both he loved them.

Chapter Thirteen

Gillian and Jenny walked along the sidewalk, Jenny talking a mile a minute about the man and how he looked mean and scary. She felt free to talk after Gillian had already identified him as well.

"The thing is," Gillian said as the approached the café, "we don't know all the facts. He did bad things, but maybe there are extenuating circumstances."

"What does that mean?" Jenny asked.

"That we need to hear his side of the story before blaming him."

"I hope he goes to jail for a long time. I could've wrecked Sally Anne's bike."

"But you didn't. And you're all right, except for a couple of scrapes. And now we are having ice cream."

Gillian opened the door with a flourish and Jenny giggled.

Marcie must have had built-in radar. No sooner were the two of them served sundaes than she came from her office to join them.

"Make me one of the same, please," she said to the waitress, who had hurried over when spotting Marcie.

"So are we celebrating something?" she asked.

"We're going to buy me a bike," Jenny said.

Marcie looked surprised, then duly impressed. "Cool, kid. How fun."

Gillian nodded. "Weird. She crashed Sally Anne's bike and the next thing I know Joe's saying he'll buy one for her. So we're going shopping, but right now Joe's with the sheriff. They caught the man who has been causing problems."

"That's such great news," Marcie said.

"Do you want to go with us to buy my bike?" Jenny asked.

Marcie looked back and forth between Jenny and Gillian. "No, I don't think I'll go. This is a special family time."

"That's what Uncle Zack said," Jenny said.

"I'm hardly family," Gillian murmured.

Marcie just shrugged and ate another bite of her sundae.

"I've been working on getting my studio ready for classes," Gillian said.

"So should I sign up for morning classes? Or afternoon or evening?" Marcie asked. They began to discuss the likelihood of women choosing different times, how crowded the classes might be. Marcie was interested in the class for seniors.

"Maybe my dad could join. He's retired and sometimes I think he's at loose ends. Though lately, I haven't seen him as much as I did a few months ago. I hope he's not becoming depressed and not leaving the house."

"That gives me a great idea. What if I sell gift certificates? Then you can get him enrolled and he'll probably come a few times just to enjoy the gift."

"Sounds like a great plan," Marcie said.

When Joe entered the café sometime later, it was crowded with early dinner customers. He quickly looked around the place but didn't see Jenny or Gillian. A waitress passing smiled at him. "Need a table, or did you come for Jenny?"

"Jenny," he said.

"She's in Marcie's office with Marcie and Gillian."

Joe headed toward the back where the office was situated.

Laughter greeted him as he opened the door. Jenny was standing between the two women, all three laughing as they stared at something on Marcie's computer screen.

"That one, you should wear that one," Jenny said, pointing. They all laughed harder.

"A private joke?" he asked.

All three looked at him in surprise. Jenny broke away and ran to him. "We're thinking up styles for Gillian's studio. Marcie's waitresses dress up, so Gillian should, too, don't you think?" She tugged at his hand. "Come and see."

Joe walked around the desk to see what was on the screen. His recent revelation made him even more aware of Gillian. Her hair was a golden red halo around her head. Her bright blue eyes held amusement as she stared at the screen. He wanted to reach out and put his hand on her shoulder just for the connection. Instead, he forced himself to look at the screen. He laughed. The costume was that of a traditional ballerina, tutu around her waist and a pink leotard and pink tights.

"Could you do aerobics in that?" he asked.

"No," Gillian said with a grin. "But it's the ambiance we're looking for."

"Like Marcie has here," Jenny explained. "I think it's beautiful."

"For a ballet. I'm thinking hard workout, plenty of movement and get-your-heart-pounding exercise."

Joe didn't know about the exercises she planned, but just being near her had his heart pounding. He wanted to know more about her, wanted to see her every day, whether tired from a hard workout or dressed for church.

He'd like to enjoy her cooking the rest of his life.

Would she ever consider sitting across the table from him at every meal?

That thought stopped him.

Were things moving too fast? He'd just realized a little while ago that he cared for Gillian, loved her. He had no way of knowing if she saw him in a similar light.

"I hate to break up such serious planning, but the store is about to close. If we want to get that bike today, we need to get a move on," Joe said.

Jenny gave Marcie a hug. "I have to go get my bike," she said with excitement.

Gillian gave her a hug as well. "I'll call you later," she promised.

Entering the sporting goods store a few moments later, Gillian was surprised at the huge array of items. She hadn't expected so many different types of sports equipment in such a small-town store. How had she missed this place in her walks through the town?

"This serves lots of summer visitors who decide they want to play beach volleyball or buy a small skiff to take on the water after they get here," Joe explained.

It was as if he picked up on her thoughts. She nodded, watching as Jenny raced over to the long row of bicycles.

"She's so excited," Gillian said, smiling up at Joe. "Thanks for including me."

"Hey, you started this, chastising me for keeping her too sheltered."

"I was not chastising you," she said.

"Okay, berating, lambasting, rebuking…"

"Ah, rebuke—I like that one. It's Bible based."

He nodded. "And you were right. You and Zack. She needs a chance to explore while she has the safety of her family around her."

"Plus, you don't want her to be the only kid in second grade without a bike. Or a horse."

"Whoa, not the horse again?"

Gillian smiled. Joe laughed.

Jenny was already sitting on a pretty pink bicycle when they reached her. "I like this one the bestest," she said.

The store owner strolled over. "Good choice, young lady. Joe, how are you? Heard about your fire. Healing okay?"

"Doing fine, Mac. Have you met Gillian Parker yet? She's staying in Sophie's home."

"Pleasure," Mac said, offering his hand. "Seen you in church a couple of times."

Gillian loved the feeling she had every time something like this happened. Before long, she'd have a nodding acquaintance with everyone in Rocky Point.

She shook his hand, mentioning her plans to open an

aerobics studio. She promised to do business exclusively with him when she needed mats and equipment.

Jenny wanted to ride her new bicycle home, but Joe refused.

"You need to show me you know how to ride one properly before trying long distances. And no riding on the road between our house and town. There are narrow shoulders and a dangerous curve. I'll bring your bike down here in the truck so you can ride in the park with your friends."

"Okay." She was jumping with happiness.

"And we still need dinner," Joe said as he placed the bike in the back of the truck.

"I don't know how hungry we'll be, after our sundaes," Gillian said.

"I'm hungry," Jenny offered.

"Me, too. Let's head for the café and order dinner. Any left over, we'll take to Zack," Joe said.

Dinner was fun. Jenny was excited about her bike and twice ran to the door of the café to make sure it was still in the back of the truck.

"Since the bad man is in jail, no one can take it," she said at one point.

Gillian met Joe's eyes, raising her eyebrows in silent question.

"Later," was all he said.

"Did you hear from Julian?" he asked at one point.

"Oh, my goodness. How could I forget? Yes. And it's mine. The house is mine! I also had an interesting meeting with my father," she replied, filling him in on the encounter.

"What do you think?"

"His bluff was about to be called and he lit out before he got caught."

"Maybe, but he said he'd like to keep in touch."

"Then I'm glad—for you."

"I'm reminded of the Scripture, 'Rejoice in the Lord always, and again I say rejoice.' We all have something to rejoice for today," Gillian said.

"You're right. But it's time to go home."

When they reached Gillian's house, Joe got out with her and walked her to the door.

"Once Jenny is in bed, would you like to walk along the bluff? It's warm enough tonight if you wear a sweater. And I can let you know what I found out about Ben," Joe suggested.

"I'd like that."

Shortly after eight, Joe knocked on the back door. Gillian grabbed her jacket and went to open it.

"It's lovely out," he said.

The sky was darkening, and bright stars were shining through. More would appear later in the dark night sky. The moon was only a sliver, giving a minuscule amount of light.

As they walked to the bluff, Joe reached for her hand, lacing their fingers and holding hers firmly in his. Gillian felt warmth surround her as they walked to the edge of the bluff and stopped, looking toward the sea. The soughing of the waves against the sand sounded like a gentle melody. She could hardly wait for summer to explore the beach and sit by the water.

"I can't wait to experience all the seasons here. In Vegas

we pretty much have hot and hotter," she said, leaning just a little against Joe.

"Wait until the middle of winter. You'll be yearning for some of that heat."

"Maybe."

Secretly, Gillian didn't think so. The warmth of friendship would be better for her soul than all the heat in Nevada.

"Tell me about Ben," she said.

They turned and began walking along the bluff. Joe gave a brief recap of the background and then Tate's interview.

"So we know the whys and wherefores. He thought your house was mine. It was mine he was trying to burn down. He was so drunk that night he could hardly stand, it sounds like."

"He has a definite problem."

"Right. His wife was angry with him for drinking so much that she threatened to leave him. He was angry with me, instead of himself. When we called her from the sheriff's office, it was the final straw. She sent Pastor John to speak with Ben, but she refused to come herself—or offer any more help. I'm not sure what she'll do. She's been a stay-at-home mother and now has her husband in jail and no income."

"I expect the church will rally around until she gets a job," Gillian said, already knowing the love and support Trinity Church offered.

They walked along in silence for a while. Gillian glanced at him from time to time, wondering at the worried look on Joe's face.

"Is there more?" she finally asked.

"No."

He stopped, and she did as well, turning to look at him.

"We haven't known each other for long," he began, his thumb gently rubbing against the back of her hand, a movement that caused her heart to jump into her throat.

"No."

Her heart began to race.

"I haven't always been the best of neighbors."

"I don't know about that. You came to my rescue more than once. You and Jenny have welcomed me into your home, shared meals and priceless stories of Sophie."

"Jenny can be tenacious sometimes."

"I love her. She's precious. Full of life and excitement to explore all it offers."

He stared at her. "How do you feel about her father?"

Gillian was surprised and took a step back until his hand tugged her closer. What should she say? What could she say without giving away her heart?

"Maybe it'll help if I tell you how Jenny's father feels about you," he said when she didn't say anything. "First, I love you for being steadfast in your love of the Lord and for reminding me that God has a plan for us all. I was lost for a time after Pamela died. But now, I'm finding my way back. I'm not all the way there, but I could be, with your help, I think. I've fallen in love with you, Gillian. I know we have lots more to learn about each other, but do you think, given enough time, you could fall for me?"

Her heart melted, and Gillian nodded. "And I wouldn't need much time at all. None, in fact. I think I've loved you since before I was even aware of it. Are you sure?"

"Never more sure of anything," Joe said, drawing her into his arms and kissing her tenderly.

When they ended the kiss, he gazed down at her.

"You've lifted a huge load from my shoulders. I felt like I'd been such a failure as a husband. But your idea that Pamela might have just wanted to force me into a vacation changes my perspective. I'm not sure I'll be the best husband in the world, but you can count on my trying my best to be just that."

"And your best will be more than enough," she said. Her heart was full to overflowing.

"Will you do me the honor of becoming my wife?" he asked, resting his forehead against hers. "We don't have to marry right away. We can get to know each other better. But I know the journey I've taken to get here and my heart's not going to change. I'll love you forever."

Gillian gazed up into his eyes, wishing again she could see him more clearly than she could in the dim illumination of the stars. She heard the sincerity of his voice, knew the truth of her own heart. This was a man she could share her life with.

I would love to marry you. And be a mother to Jenny."

"Amen to that. We'll have the life the Lord laid out for us, together, making a family, making memories to sustain us all our lives."

"I've been praying you might see me in just such a light."

"Oh, you have, have you?" He kissed her lightly. "Jenny will be thrilled."

"I hope so. I love her so much. I'd like to have some

children together, too."

"So would I. Let's fill our home with love and laughter and devotion to God."

Gillian hugged him tightly, savoring the blossoming contentment that filled her heart. She'd finally found the place she was meant to be thanks to the wonderful legacy her great-grandmother has left her.

Did you enjoy this story? If so you may enjoy
Rocky Point Box Set Books 4-6 or ***Rocky Point Reunion***

More books by Barbara McMahon

The Harts of Texas Series
Rebel Heart
Tangled Hearts
Reckless Heart

Cowboy Heroes Series
The Cowboy Next Door
Cowboy's Bride
One Stubborn Cowboy
Crazy About a Cowboy
Never Doubt a Cowboy
Cowboy Marshal
Summer Cowboy
Second Chance Cowboy
Movie Star Cowboy

Tropical Escape Series
Island Rendezvous
Come into the Sun
Island Paradise
Destination Romance Boxed Set

Rocky Point Series
Rocky Point Legacy
Rocky Point Reunion
Rocky Point Promise
Rocky Point Hero
Rocky Point Inn
Rocky Point Dawn

Elite Security Mystery Series
Trusting Jake

The Ultimate Billionaires
The Cynical Sheikh
Falling for the Sheikh
A Sheikh of Her Own
The Unforgettable Sheikh

Other Books
A Soldier's Christmas
I'll Take Forever
Jared's Promise
The Paper Marriage
The Christmas Locket
The Banished Bride
Cowboy Charade
The Cowboy's Special Christmas
Mail Order Bride
Because of You
Sweet Meant To Be